SECURING THE BAG AND HIS HEART TOO

KYEATE

ACKNOWLEDGMENTS

Another one of these huh? First and Foremost, I would like to thank God for allowing me to make it this far with the talent of being a writer. Writing started off as being a piece of cake, but I can't lie and say that it hasn't got hard. The urge to give up has come and gone on plenty of occasions but it did not win.

J.A.Z- my three amigos, thank you guys for allowing mommy to be an inspiration for your future endeavors and school projects. You guys are my everything. Jon Jon, thank you son for letting me use your name for a character in this book.

My grandparents Liz and Stacey thanks for being the best to ever do it period. I can't thank y'all enough my ass will be thanking you in every book I ever write, lol.

My father and little brother Delaunn, thanks for letting me use your name in this book. I'm so sorry for making your character an asswipe. I love y'all!!

To my little sister Tammara who has supported me since day one and has a feature in this book. I love you, Key-Lolo

To my pen sisters, thank you guys for being that motivation and being something that a girl can look up to. I love every one of y'all.

To my dope ass publisher Mz. Lady P, I humbly thank you for

giving me this chance. I thank you for the motivational speeches when I was about to give up. I thank you for the learning experiences as I continue.

Knock me down nine times but I get up ten
Look myself in the mirror, I say we gone win
~Cardi B

CONNECT WITH KYEATE

Facebook: Kyeate Holt, Kyeate's Book Club, Kye Writez
Instagram: KyeWritez
Twitter: Adjustnmykrown

Be sure to follow Kyeate's Book Club and Kye Writez for updates on new releases.

PREVIOUSLY IN SECURING THE BAG AND HIS HEART

Muza Entertainment 3rd Annual Ball

It was the day of my annual ball, and before I started running around like a chicken with my head cut off and doing interviews and photo ops, I had to make a very important stop. I stood there thinking about what I was about to do, and it took a lot of long nights and fighting with myself to bring me to this point. Lifting my hand, I knocked on the door and waited patiently. To calm my nerves, I couldn't find shit to do with my hands, so I placed them in my pocket of the pants I had on. The door opened, and there she stood looking like a goddess.

"What's up?" Nova asked.

Just hearing her voice did something to me. I know it's been a week, but it felt like years. She stood there wearing a pair of shorts and a sports bra and had her locs in a high bun on her head.

"Look before you flip out on me, I'm sorry for popping up at your spot, but I was heading to the venue, and I wanted to do this face to face. I know we have a lot to talk about, which we will get to all that, but I sort of don't have the time right now. I wanted to apologize for spazzing out on you and asking you to leave. I understand I was wrong, and I should've believed you wouldn't do anything like that. As you know, tonight is my annual ball, and

before all this shit happened, I was going to take you as my date. If you say yes, my stylist is downstairs and ready to take you to handle everything you need to do in preparation for tonight. Nova, will you please do me the honor of escorting me to the ball tonight?" I asked. I could tell she was stunned.

"Muza, we really do have a lot to talk about, but yes I will go with you tonight," she said. Hearing her say yes was music to my ears. I leaned in and placed a kiss on her cheek.

"Thank you. I have to run but get dressed, and a car is waiting for you downstairs," I told her. This shit was going to be great. I went back to the car and headed to my first stop.

I knew the step I was taking tonight was a huge one, but being away from Nova the way that we were, I knew that I loved her and wanted to spend the rest of my life showing her. I just pray that she felt the same way about me and can forgive me for the way that I handled that little shit.

NOVA

To open my door and see Muza standing there looking fine as ever, I was shocked but happy at the same time. So, hearing that he wanted me to go to the ball with him was all I needed to get my foot back in the door and get things back on track with my baby daddy. I knew he had someone waiting on me, and I didn't want to keep them waiting long, so I threw on a pair of Victoria Secret PINK yoga pants with a matching top, grabbed my bag, and headed downstairs to the car.

"Sorry for taking so long," I said once I got inside the car. The stylist seemed cool.

"It's ok. I'm on your time. Well, we do have to have you ready before a certain time, but Mr. Muhammad has everything set for you. While you're getting your hair done, I will show you a few pieces that we had flown in, and you can narrow the choices down from there. Also, you will be getting your nails and feet done during your hair process. My name is Tammara by the way," she spoke rarely making eye contact. She had her face glued to her phone and tablet.

"Cool, sounds like a plan, I know getting this head of mine done can take some time," I told her. She finally looked up.

"I'm sorry, I had to make sure Mr. Muhammad suit is just right. As you

1

know I'm his stylist, and I also handle the designs for his clothing line, so you may find me working on three things at once," Tammara said taking a sip of the energy drink she had. I laughed she was wired.

The first stop we made was to the salon. Once inside I was treated like royalty. Baby the way my head was washed, I'm sure I came on myself. While the re-twisting process began everything that Tammara told me about started to happen. In she rolled a big ass rack full of dresses and there was so many to choose from. I swear I could get used to this type of treatment.

"I'll show you a dress, and you say yay or nay then we can go from there," Tammara said, holding up the first dress.

I know I shook my head to the first five dresses she held up, and then the next one she held up I knew it was the one. It was giving me Rihanna and Cardi B vibes.

"That's it. I don't need to see anymore. I want that one," I told Tammara. She nodded her head.

"Ok, I see you got taste. This is an Alexander McQueen," she said. This dress was everything it was a petal pink midi knitted dress with a vintage corset like bustier top. The dress had grosgrain details on the shoulder straps with a metal adjuster and metal zipper fastening on the center front. This shit was bad.

After Tammara left to get my shoes, the lady finished up my hair. Then I was off to makeup. I couldn't believe I had been here almost five damn hours. A bitch was sleepy and hungry, but I was scared to eat anything because this child of mine wouldn't let it digest. I was literally snacking on crackers and ginger ale, which was pissing me off even more.

"You ready to see yourself?" Tammara asked while standing behind me.

"Yes, I'm nervous though," I admitted.

"Don't be because girl you are finnne, and you are rocking the hell out of that dress," she said. I slowly turned around, and my mouth flew open I knew I was the shit, but damn.

"Lord, I swear all our problems gone go away when he sees me in this dress," I admitted. Tammara laughed.

"I don't know much about you, but I can tell Muza genuinely cares for you. I can vibe with you. That Cru wench he used to date, this is so unprofes-

2

sional of me, but I couldn't stand that bitch and the broom she flew in on," Tammara admitted. I busted out laughing

"Yeah, she a mess. Thank you for helping me today," I told her leaning in and hugging her.

"Let's get you to your man because I know he is waiting on you, boo," she said, and we both walked back to the car.

MUZA

*L*ooking down at my watch, I was watching the time like a hawk. Nova should've been here by now. A nigga was nervous hoping she ain't back out on a nigga. The majority of all the interviews that I had done so far today was asking about Nova and the baby. I swear living the life I lived, a nigga had no privacy thanks to the paparazzi. It was almost time for me to walk the red carpet. I spotted my Maybach pulling up, and I noticed it was my driver. Walking down the steps, I headed to the carpet and waited for the car to come to a complete stop. My driver got out and made his way to the back of the car, opening the door there she was.

"Damn," I mouthed.

Nova looked like she was made to be beside me. I mean I honestly didn't have any words to speak, she was breathtaking. I swallowed the lump in my throat and placed my hand out for her to grab.

"Girl, you so damn fine," I told her. She was blushing so damn hard.

"Thank you for all of this and thanks for the compliment," she said.

"Well, I know you a natural and shit, but are you ready to hit this red carpet because every damn interview I did today I was asked Where is Nova and questions about the baby, so you gone get bombarded," I told her.

"I'm fine. It's nothing I can't handle," she answered. I placed my hand on the small of her back, and we made our way to the red carpet.

The cameras were flashing, and Nova was working that shit like she always did. Each mic we stopped at asked us the infamous questions about the baby and our relationship. Nova shocked me when she told them that we were expecting, but she wanted that part of her life to remain private until she was ready to share certain aspects of it with the world. She did better than I would have. She was early in her pregnancy, so she didn't want to give out too much too soon, and something happened, so I understood that fully because I didn't want anything to happen to my baby. It was some shit most pregnant women lived by, so I could dig it.

We finally made our way inside after a good thirty minutes of interviews and photos. Nova didn't leave my side. I told her she could mingle, but she wanted to be right by me. Malcolm and my aunt had made their way over to us, and we started laughing and talking. Nova and Elizabeth were talking about the pregnancy and Unc and I was chopping it up about the announcement that I was going to make tonight.

"Ahem!" we heard, and we all turned around staring at Cru and Delaunn. I knew my ass should've put out a ban list for the event.

Nova walked over to me and stood beside me to make her presence known.

"What do you want Cru, and if you try any shit I will throw your ass out of this party so fast," I said through gritted teeth, but making sure to keep calm because I knew cameras were on me always.

"You don't have to be so rude. I was only coming by to congratulate you both on your child. I can honestly say I'm happy for you," she had the nerve to say, causing me to raise my eyebrow. I couldn't help but notice the look that Delaunn was giving Nova, and she was looking dead at Cru.

"Thank you. Stick around it's more to congratulate on," I told her, walking past her and Delaunn taking Nova with me. Malcolm and my aunt followed.

"Come on stage with me. I have to introduce the performers," I told Nova.

"Ok!" she said excitedly. Walking up on the stage, I grabbed the mic as the crowd cheered us on.

"Thank you, guys, for coming out tonight and thank those that have supported this event every year. As you guys know all donations from this event goes to the Women's Foundation for those who suffer from drug abuse,

physical abuse, or just need help period. I have dedicated my life to this because of my mother. A lot of y'all have been asking about this lady right here, and yes, she holds a special part of me. A piece of me that I've always wanted. That's why I can only do what's right and pray that she will accept what I'm about to do," I spoke to the crowd as they cheered on.

I reached into my pocket and got down on one knee. Nova was shaking her head, and everyone was screaming. I spoke into the mic

"Novanna Collier, will you marry me?" I asked. Loud moans came over the loudspeaker catching me off guard. I turned around, and there was a video on the screen of Nova and Delaunn fucking.

"Oh my god!" Nova cried.

"Turn that shit off right now!" I yelled. Everyone had their phones out recording.

"Don't tape that shit!" I yelled. Nova ran off stage, and I followed behind her. She ran dead smack into Cru and Delaunn who were both wearing mischievous grins.

"Oh, what was that other congrats you were talking about?" Delaunn asked. I reached behind Nova and rocked his ass to sleep while Nova had pounced on Cru.

"Worldstar!" I heard someone yell.

NOVA

"*Get the fuck off me!*" *I yelled as my father was pulling me off Cru. This bitch had just ruined my life in the worse way.*

"Come on baby girl, you pregnant," Malcolm calmly said, pulling me away. I looked over at Muza who had a look of pure hatred on his face.

"It's not what you think Muza," I told him.

"It's not what I think. Y'all just made a fool out of me. Here I am proposing to you because I wanted to spend the rest of my life with you, and you all on video fucking the next nigga. Everyone has seen this shit, and this shit is gone be in every paper and all over social media. Fuck!" he yelled.

My emotions were getting the best of me. I couldn't stop crying long enough to even get my words out.

"I swear it's nothing between him and me," I cried.

"That's what you say. Hell, is that even my baby you are carrying or that nigga's?" Muza asked.

"Really Muza?" I cried.

"You know what fuck this shit. This right here between us is over, and all that shit I said on stage you can forget that shit," he said tossing the ring in the trash and walking away. Tammara ran over to the trash can and reached in and got the ring.

"This nigga is crazy," she said. Looking at the box, I just fell in my daddy's arms and cried.

"This isn't fair daddy. That video is so old. I told you he was crazy," I said. Malcolm caressed my back.

"It's ok we will get through this like we get through everything else," he reassured me.

I wasn't so sure about this though. This was damaging to the both of us. I felt so bad for Muza, and the worst part is I hadn't even had a chance to tell him my secret yet. I knew for a fact he would never want my ass then. Cru and Delaunn were gone see me, and I put that on my unborn.

Muzaini

I HAD NEVER BEEN SO HUMILIATED in my life. Here I was bragging about the woman I love and wanting to make her my wife, but it was apparent that Nova had other things on her mind. Seeing her being fucked by that nigga ignited a fire in me that I wasn't sure I could control. I was hurt, and I'm that nigga, so that was not a good look. It has been two weeks since that shit went down, and I had my people doing damage control, trying to get my ass out of the spotlight. The media was having a field day with it. Somehow, they all wanted to interview Nova, and I hadn't spoken with her, but what she put out for everyone to know did kind of spin the whole thing, and now everyone was attacking Delaunn and Cru.

Nova had told them that Cru and Delaunn were salty about our relationship being the bitter exes, and it was them that tried to leak an old video that she didn't even know was being recorded. Last I heard, she was pressing charges against Delaunn. I didn't let that shit change my life. I just put myself in my work.

"Mr. Muhammad, you have a visitor," my secretary's voice came through the speaker.

"Who is it?" I asked.

"Umm sir, it's Cru. Do you want me to ask her to leave?" she hesitated. Letting out a huge sigh, I wasn't sure if I even wanted to speak with her. Her ass had been blowing me up since the party, and I don't know why.

"Send her back," I told her. I scooted back in my chair and placed my hands on my stomach and waited for her to make her entrance. When the door opened, and she walked in, I couldn't do nothing but shake my head. Maybe it was because a nigga ain't had none in awhile, but damn she was fine. The long jumbo braids she rocked looked nice touching her ass. She showcased her smile that used to have a nigga weak. I kept my poker face on though I didn't want her to know the effect she was having on me.

"I'm surprised that you actually let me come back. I have been reaching out to you," she said, taking a seat.

"I don't know what you are reaching out for. You have caused enough damage in my life," I told her, and it wasn't nothing but the truth.

"Muzaini, all I did was keep you from making a huge mistake. Nova was just about the money. Delaunn told me everything about their relationship, and soon as she seen a bigger payday in you, you know what she did? She dropped him like a bad habit. Are you sure you wanted to marry her? Granted she is possibly carrying your child, and I know that was something you always wanted, but I love you, Muza. I really do, and I couldn't allow that to happen. Now she is spreading these rumors about me like I had something to do with the tape, but that was all Delaunn's doing," Cru spilled.

"If all you were doing was trying to keep me from making a mistake, why didn't you come to me personally, Cru? If you knew this nigga was going to do some bogus shit like he did, why you ain't talk him out of that?" I asked her. I kind of was getting what Cru was saying, but some shit just wasn't adding up.

"Honestly, I didn't. He told me he was going to come and talk to you like a man because he didn't know if the baby was his or not because Nova wasn't speaking to him. I simply was in the wrong place at the wrong time," she said.

"Guilty by association," I told her. Cru stood up and walked behind the desk and stood in front of me.

"Muza, I know that I messed up while we together, but I really love you, and I'm willing to make some changes to prove to you just how much I love you," she said.

I looked at her, and at that moment, my head wasn't thinking straight, but my other head was wanting to do all the talking.

"Show me," I said, unzipping my pants.

Cru dropped to her knees and went to work. I closed my eyes and enjoyed the warmth of her mouth. I knew dealing with Cru's crazy ass that I shouldn't even be doing this because now a nigga wouldn't be able to get rid of her. My heart was still with Nova, and I couldn't shake that shit.

NOVA

"Thank you, I will see you Monday morning," I told my lawyer and hung up the phone.

Things for me have been a pain since the night of Muza's ball consisting of many interviews and being bothered or harassed on social media. I was the victim in all of this, and that's why I was going through with pressing charges on Delaunn. What he did was something they call revenge porn, and it was a law that they took seriously in Tennessee.

I missed Muza more than anything, but I knew that it was over for us. The only concern he had was this child I was carrying, even though I wasn't going to be harassing him about that either. He wanted to question if he was the father or not, so I was going to give him a paternity test and gone on about my business. I closed my laptop. I was done with writing for the day. I submitted the first couple chapters of a book to Mz. Lady P and I was waiting on a response. I was moving forward in my life. There was a knock at the door, and I stood up to go get it. Looking through the peephole, I saw that it was Kelly. Sucking my teeth, I opened the door.

"What?" I asked. I wasn't here for her shit, and I most definitely wasn't fucking with her trick ass no more.

"I just came to get my stuff," she said, looking at the floor.

"You got you half of the rent?" I asked, I wasn't hurting for no damn rent money, but this bitch was gone pay.

"What you mean?" she asked.

"I do recall you staying here, and you just left without paying the rent. If you got money, you could get your stuff," I told her, crossing my arms.

"I only have two hundred dollars, Nova," she said, reaching into her bag.

I closed the door, walked to her room, and grabbed two trash bags not even looking inside to see what the contents were. Walking back to the door, I opened the door and sat the two bags at her feet.

"Two hundred dollars for two bags; you'll get the rest when you have the rest of my money," I told her, holding my hand out.

"I swear you're a bitch," she said.

"I'm a paid bitch. You did me so dirty you're lucky I'm even entertaining your fake ass right now. Get the fuck off my doorstep," I told her.

"How did that engagement go? You just wait I got you," she said. My antennas went up to the shit my father told me a minute ago about her ass.

"Bitch, get out!" I said, closing the door in her face. That hoe was going to be a problem.

Jon Jon

A NIGGA WAS CHILLING and enjoying the fruits of my labor. I had moved into a bigger spot since Kelly had come back and told me she was pregnant. A nigga didn't want no damn kids no time soon, but shit, as long as I could keep her ass around so that she wouldn't open her mouth, then the shit was aite I guess. Smoking from the blunt that I just rolled up, I let the smoke feel my lungs. Kelly walked in and dropped two trash bags on the floor. I lifted my head off the couch and looked at her like she was crazy.

"Yo, what is that shit?" I asked clearly pissed off.

"Some of my shit. You know that bitch made me pay her for this shit. She told me I could get the rest of my stuff when I bring the rest of her money," Kelly said, plopping down on the couch.

"You need to get that shit out the middle of my floor. What money you owe her?" I asked.

"Rent," she said.

"Oh. I guess you need to pay that before she takes that ass to court," I told her hitting the blunt again. I blew the smoke in Kelly's face.

"Really Jon Jon, where I'm gone get the money from?" she asked me.

"I don't know, but you need to get them damn bags out the middle of the floor like I asked. I'm not going to repeat myself," I said in a more serious tone.

Kelly jumped up, snatched the bags, and headed out of the room. I laughed because I was just fucking with her ass, I loved getting under her skin. She left my ass alone when she thought I was mad at her.

MUZAINI

a nigga had fucked up big time. I end up fucking Cru damn ass in my office. I was gone stop at the head, but shit, I couldn't resist. My judgment was cloudy, and she offered to come over and cook dinner, and my damn dumb ass agreed. I felt bad as fuck. Was that normal considering I'm single, but I felt like I cheated on Nova. I needed to get some things off my chest and I felt now was the time.

I pulled up to Nova's apartment, and I just sat there for a minute. I had gassed myself to come over here and talk. What did I want to know? What could she possibly tell me that was different from what I had already heard? I closed my eyes and let out a deep breath because I was going to have to face her sooner or later. I couldn't ignore this like the shit hadn't happened. I slowly opened the door, getting out of the car. I placed my shades on my face so that she couldn't read me and skipped upstairs to her apartment. It was now or never, so I knocked on the door.

"Who is it?" I heard her yell.

"Muza!" I responded. There was a pause for what I know to be about two minutes, and then I heard the locks on the door. Nova opened the door, and shit, I was speechless.

"Um, hello?" I heard her say, snapping me out of my trance, I looked at her up and down, taking in her beauty.

"My bad, is it ok if I come in? I think it's time we talk," I asked her.

Nova crossed her arms and moved to the side, letting me in. I walked in and went straight to the living room, taking a seat on the couch, which I noticed was new. I looked around the place, and literally everything had been replaced.

"I like what you did with the place," I said.

She took a seat at one of the bar stools that were in front of the bar area and looked at me as if I was bothering her.

"It comes a time in life when things need to be replaced— ALL things," she said, emphasizing the all. I caught every bit of that shade.

"You're right about that. I think a conversation deserves to be had about the things that took place that night at the ball. I know things have been overwhelming for the both of us, but it seems like we still have to deal with each other," I said, pointing to Nova's stomach.

"Before we talk remove your shades, and you know I was waiting for this day to come because this is the norm for you. You run away from situations until you're ready to deal with them, but this whole time I have been dealing with this shit. I was the victim in all of this. You were just embarrassed as you say. Like I was trying to tell you from the jump, that video was old, and I didn't even know I was being recorded. Matter of fact, you remember the day you were sitting outside of my apartment stalking me, and I came home? You told me about keeping it real with you because you knew I was hiding something. That was the same day and the last time that I was ever with him. I never cheated on you, and what hurts the most is you had the nerve to question my child as if I lied to you about that. Now don't get me wrong when I found out I was pregnant I questioned myself, but Delaunn never came in me, so I knew then that this baby was yours. The damage has been done, and everyone has seen me in my most private form. Meanwhile, all you're worried about is your name," she said. I could tell she was hurt and had an attitude.

"What do you expect? A lot of things have happened since we tried this relationship thing. First the robbery and then this shit. I'm like damn can I really marry you?" I told her, regretting how I worded that shit the instant it left my mouth.

"And like I told you the first time I didn't have shit to do with that robbery. Like your ass don't know by now that that shit was Kelly and Jon Jon's doing. I mean it's cool you don't trust me and that you may look at me differently because I see some people must have got in your head, and most likely it was a hating ass bitch. Muza, hear me and hear me well when I tell you this. Me and you will never work because this shit will forever be on your mind. Again, it's clear you don't trust me. I just wish that you could see I was always loyal to you and faithful from the day we got together. I love you, but I love me more, and no matter how bad I hate that we have come to this, I will not chase you nor beg you to be with me. If you want a paternity test when the baby is born, you can have that also," she said.

Wait a damn minute she wasn't supposed to be handling this as good as she was.

"So, why aren't you gone tell me the truth about you and Delaunn?" I asked. I wanted to fish around about the shit Cru told me.

"What the hell does he have to do with us? I told you all that happened. He's just a bitter ass nigga," she said.

"So, you weren't with him for his money and then when you met me, a bigger payday, you hopped on me and left that nigga out in the cold like that. That's why he was tripping, but hell, who wouldn't? You can't play with people feelings like that, Nova," I said.

For some reason I wanted her to hurt like I was hurting. If I couldn't be happy, why should she be able to be happy?

"You know what how I met Delaunn and what we had going on isn't your business anymore because we are not together, engaged, or none of that. You're tripping real hard. I thought this would be a civilized conversation, but I see now this is over," she said.

"It must be true. I'll go, but before I do I just need you to know that I will be there for my child, so I need to know about all appointments and shit like that, and you also need to get prepared for Cru to be in the picture once the baby is born," I said.

"Wait hold on, why do I need to be prepared for that?" she asked, placing her hands on her hip.

"We are back together now," I said, walking towards the door.

"How can you be with someone who played a part in that shit that happened at the ball?" she asked.

"She didn't. She was tryna warn me about the gold digging chick that I was about to marry. Speaking of which, I think Kelly called you the same thing. What was it, a money hungry dick jumping hoe?" I told her. I knew I was wrong and my face felt every bit of the punch that followed.

"Are you fucking crazy?" I yelled.

"No, but you are. Get the fuck out of my house before I black your other eye!" Nova yelled.

I knew I fucked up, and I asked for that shit.

NOVANNA

J was so turned up that I was pacing the floor like Yvette on *Baby Boy* right before Jody knocked her ass out. This nigga had me messed up. I wanted to cry because this wasn't Muza. I just knew Cru had gotten in his head. It wasn't nobody else but her. I laughed at the fact that I had punched Muza in his eye, I'm glad his ass ain't have no reflex.

My ass was hungry, so I headed to the kitchen and grabbed me some pickles and Chester's Hot Fries to satisfy my craving. My phone rang, and I grabbed it. It was my dad Malcolm FaceTiming me.

"What's up, Pops?" I said, looking into the phone taking a bite of my pickle.

"Nova, why you over there putting your hands on folks?" he asked. I shook my head. This nigga had the nerve to tell on me.

"Man, he was disrespectful as hell. I ain't never took no shit from nobody, and I'm not about to start letting him think he can disrespect me. Did you know that he and Cru are back together?" I asked him.

"No, I didn't. Who told you that?" he asked.

"He did that was before he called me a money hungry dick hopping hoe," I said. My father's face changed like he was instantly pissed.

"He let that girl fill his head up with bullshit. I don't care what she says. I know she played a part with Delaunn and that shit he pulled. Then he got the nerve to be laying up with her talking about get used to her being around my baby. He got me fucked up, daddy. I will put my Louboutin on that hoe's neck if she thinks she gone play with me," I told him.

"Nova, calm down and don't get all stressed out with my grandchild. I'm gone have a talk with him because he ain't think to tell me all that shit. Did you tell him about you know what?" he asked, referring to my escorting.

"No, I didn't, and what's the point now. It's done between us," I mumbled.

"Communication is key. Yeah, he's mad right now, but he's gone be even madder when he hears it from somebody else rather than from you all this time. I'm just trying to tell you," Malcolm said.

"I understand. Well, I'm about to finish my snack. Tell Elizabeth I said hi, and I will talk to you guys later.

"Aite then, love you, baby girl," he said. I laid the phone down and continued to eat my snack.

CRU

I was walking around on cloud nine. I had stopped by my house to pick up a few items before heading over to Muza's. Things were finally going to get back to how they use to be. I knew once I broke him off some and planted that seed in his head about Nova that he would come running back. *Manifest in your life sis and watch it become what you want* was what I lived by. Grabbing my overnight bag, I flew out the door and headed to my man.

I hopped in my Telsa and turned on my boo Ella Mai banging "Boo'd Up" the whole drive to Muza's

Ooh, now I'll never get over you until I find something new
That get me high like you do, yeah yeah
Ooh, now I'll never get over you until I find something new
That get me high like you do
Listen to my heart go ba-dum, boo'd up
Biddy-da-dum, boo'd up

PULLING into the driveway Muza's cars were lined up, and I pulled right behind one. I checked my makeup and adjusted my breasts as I got out the car, making my way up the steps. I ranged the doorbell while checking my clothes, making sure I looked nice. The door opened, and my mouth dropped.

"What happened to your eye?" I gasped.

"Nova is what happened," he said, letting me in.

"What the fuck, Muza? You should have her ass locked up. She shouldn't be putting her hands on you," I told him. We walked in the kitchen, and I looked at his eye.

"Ain't nobody about to press charges on her. Shit just got emotional, and I said some fucked up shit," he said.

"That doesn't justify her putting her hands on you. Let that had been you blacking her eye, and you wouldn't be sitting her talking to me right now because you would be in jail," I told him. He stood up from the table.

"Look, just cook whatever it is you were about to cook. This conversation is over," he said, walking upstairs.

This nigga had to be in his feelings about Nova. I wasn't no dummy, and I knew he still cared for her very much, but I was just going to have to take his mind off her. It was nothing if I gave him everything he wanted.

I walked over to the refrigerator and pulled out the things that I requested his shopper to get for dinner. Usually, Muza had his meals cooked by his staff, but I wanted him to have a home cooked meal from the heart. One thing about me even though I rarely cooked because you wouldn't dare catch me in the kitchen, I could get down. I pulled out the pork chops and rinsed them off seasoning and battering them ready to drop in the fryer. While the chops fried, I peeled the potatoes and made some homemade mashed potatoes along with some green beans and gravy for the mashed potatoes and pork chops. After everything was done, I fixed Muza a plate, grabbed him a beer, and carried his plate upstairs.

When I walked in the room, Muza was sitting up in the bed going through his phone.

"I brought you your plate," I said, causing him to hurry up and put his phone down. *I wonder what the hell he was up to.*

"Thank you, Cru, and you cooked my favorite. I'm about to fuck

21

this shit up," he said, reaching for the tray. After saying a quick prayer, he dug in. I climbed into bed beside him and clicked on the tv.

"Girl, you keep cooking like this and a nigga might just keep you around," he said with a mouth full of food.

"Damn, I thought I was good enough to keep around without the food. Muza, I really hope you give me another chance. I promise you won't be disappointed," I told him.

He looked at me like he was thinking about what to say next. He placed his fork down on his plate and looked at me. His brown eyes carried a sadness as he licked his perfect lips.

"You are aware that I do have a kid on the way. I know I'm the father of Nova's baby, and I'm not about to be no deadbeat. I let your ass feed me some bullshit earlier, and I said some things to her that wasn't cool, and it might mess up our parenting relationship. That can't happen because she will be around, and hopefully if I decide to be with you for the long run, you have to respect the mother of my child," he said. What the hell did he mean *if* he decides to be with me for the long run?

"What exactly do you mean by if you decide to be with me for the long run?" I asked.

"Cru, my girl, we can't just pick up where we left off because we left off on bad terms. You're on like a trial run," he said. This nigga had me ready to flip his whole plate over on his ass, but I kept my cool.

"It's cool. You will see this is the right decision in the long run," I told him, feeling confident.

NOVANNA

Eight Months Later

My pregnancy was at the end of the road, and I was miserable as shit. This child had turned me into the biggest bitch ever. I was always irritable and snapping off on motherfuckers. I couldn't wait to push this child out. I kept my end of the deal by allowing Muza to come to all doctor appointments to keep him in the loop and that was it. I still loved him of course, but I had lost some respect for him after that blow up we had in my apartment. We literally met at the doctor office, and after the appointments, we would go our separate ways. Sometimes he did try to reach out, but I shut that shit down. I knew that he and Cru was an official item again because they asses were all over the entertainment headlines. When it first made headlines, I use to see shit like SHE WON. No bitch, I let you borrow him I use to scream.

Delaunn and I ended up settling out of court, and I was awarded 1.2 million dollars simply because he admitted to setting up the camera and recording me without permission with the intent to use for revenge purposes. The video went viral and was shared amongst many social media sites, so that helped also. I bet he thinks twice about doing some shit like that again. Delaunn was suspended from the team and probably wasn't going to be signed for another season with the Titans. I ended up moving out of that damn apartment and buying me a house. It's nothing huge but big enough for my baby and me. My dad had his friends set everything up, and Muza hired somebody to do the nursery.

I had also heard something back from my book submission, and your girl was signed to Mz. Lady P Presents. It was a feeling that I couldn't explain because I stepped out on faith and turned a dream into reality. I had a lot of time on my hands, so I spent the majority of my time writing anyways. I eased up from my desk and walked out of my office to head to the kitchen and get me some ice. I heard the front door open, and I rolled my eyes, I should've thought twice about giving my father and Elizabeth a key. Elizabeth turned the corner carrying a bag.

"Well look at you looking like you're ready to pop. I was just in the area, and I thought of you," she said, placing the bag on the counter.

"What did you bring me this time, Elizabeth?" I asked, filling my cup up with ice.

"Oh, don't act like you don't like my surprises or me popping up over here," she said, reaching into the bag and pulling out two frames. I damn near choked on my ice.

"Elizabeth what is this and what will possess you to get something like this done?" I asked, grabbing both frames.

This lady was crazy. She had gotten two pics that Muza and I had taken together the first night we went out and the night of his ball blown up in black and white and placed in a golden frame.

"This is for the baby. It has to have something to look at. Maybe it will send a blessing over this house because this is what is supposed to be. I can't believe you are sitting around here and letting him date that Cru wench and parade her around like that. What happened to fighting for your man?" she asked.

I knew it was coming. It never failed. Elizabeth always made it her point to try and talk me into some bullshit.

"Ms. Elizabeth I've told you time and time again that I'm cool on him. If that's what he wants, then he can have that. I will always love him just from a distance," I told her.

"Bullshit, I like to see the two of you try and co-parent with both of y'all still having feelings for each other. It's just a big ass mess if you ask me," she said.

"How you know he still has feelings for me?" I asked.

"He is my nephew. Do you think I just be over here harassing just you? He gets it too," Ms. Elizabeth said.

She grabbed the frames and went upstairs to the nursery, and I followed. Walking up the steps, I felt a trickle of water run down my legs then a big gush.

"Ooooh My God!" I slowly yelled.

"What. girl?" Ms. Elizabeth turned around. I looked at the ground then up at her.

"Oh, hell. Ok, let's get you back downstairs and let me call your father and Muza. Do you have a bag packed?" she asked. I nodded my head yes.

"It's a small suitcase in the nursery beside the dresser," I told her. I was keeping calm and trying not to panic because I was controlling the level of my pain. Elizabeth came back downstairs with the suitcase.

"Muza and your father will meet us at the hospital," she said, helping me off the couch. I had started doing my breathing that I had learned in Lamaze the whole walk to the car. It was time, and I was about to become someone's mother.

When we got to the hospital, Muza was waiting at the entrance with a wheelchair.

"Come on, Nova. How are you doing? You in any pain?" he asked. I could tell he was nervous.

"I'm fine. The contractions are coming more and more though," I blew. I was pushed upstairs to a private suite, where I got comfortable and waited on the arrival of my bundle of joy.

I was given an epidural and decided that I would try and get some rest because I haven't dilated fully yet. Muza was sitting by my side, and my father and Ms. Elizabeth were sitting in the corner knocked out. I felt like I was being stared at, so I opened my eyes, and Muza had his eyes locked on me.

"Why are you staring at me?" I asked, rolling my eyes.

"I'm just thinking. I wish we could've enjoyed this pregnancy together. I feel like I missed a lot. You know like being able to rub your stomach and run out and get your cravings. That's how it was supposed to be," he had the audacity to say.

"Well, it wasn't my fault. You could've had all that had you not let all the bullshit interfere or let your girlfriend Cru get in your head. I told you the truth from the start about the Delaunn situation right then, and there we could've fixed the issue and moved forward, but nah we didn't, so now we here," I told him.

"I know you still got feelings for me, Nova, no matter how you try to play it," he said.

I chuckled.

"And I know you still got feelings for me while you over there playing with Cru's head. Do you really want to be with her Muza? Or is this a get back thing?" I asked because I had to know.

"I don't know what it is, but I do have feelings for you and always will," he said. That wasn't good enough for me. I rolled over and turned my back to him.

"Don't do that me, Nova. Don't shut me out like you been doing? We can't keep doing this," he said. He was right we couldn't.

"If you don't want to be shut out, back out of that shit you got going on with Cru and come back to your family. If you can't do that, then it really isn't nothing left to discuss," I told him, and I meant every word. I felt like I started feeling pressure in my bottom.

"I think it's time," I told him. A nurse walked in as soon as I said that,.

"I noticed a spike on your monitor, I'm going to check you," she said, lifting the covers.

"Whatever you do, I know you may feel some pressure in your bottom, but do not push. I'm paging the doctor," she spoke and ran out of the room. My father stood up.

"I'm gone step outside. I don't want to see all that," he said.

"Oh, Malcolm, you are such a wuss. It's natural," Elizabeth said.

"I'm good. As soon as I hear cries, I will step back in. Good luck baby girl, you got this," he said, kissing my forehead.

Ms. Elizabeth was on one side of the bed, and Muza was on the other. The doctor came in and put his gloves on, and as soon as he lifted the sheet, his eyes widened. The nurse nodded her head.

"I told you," she said. I started to panic not knowing what the hell was going on.

"What's wrong?" I asked. The doctor looked up.

"Ok, I'm going to need you to give me one big push. You guys hold her legs if you want to. Your baby is right here, that's why you feel the urge to push. On the count of three, you're going to push. One, two, three, push!!" he said, and I did just that. I pushed with all my might.

"Give me another one," the doctor said. I pushed down until I damn near passed out, and I heard the cries of my baby.

"It's a girl!" he said.

They handed me my baby, placing her on my chest, and I was in love. Muza leaned over with tears in his eyes.

"Oh my god Nova, she is beautiful. You did a great job. Thank you for her," Muza said. My father entered the room and walked over to stand beside Ms. Elizabeth who was already taking a thousand pictures.

"This princess needs a name," she said excitedly. I looked at Muza, and we looked at our daughter.

"Star Mona Lise Muhammad," I said. It was official. She was my shining star.

MUZAINI

*M*an seeing Nova boss up and give birth to my daughter like a champ made me fall in love with her even more. The conversation we were having before she made her grand entrance was her giving me a chance to make my decision. The way my daughter was trying to come out was a sign. I was going to end things with Cru and get back with Nova. It was only right.

My Uncle Malcolm had given me a cigar with a pink ribbon, and we snapped it up while I held my baby girl.

"I think I made my decision, Unc. I'm gone get back with Nova," I told him.

"I'm proud of you making the right decision. Have you guys had a chance to really talk about everything?" he asked.

"I mean yeah we discussed some stuff. I just got to talk to Cru, and she ain't gone take this too well. I need to run downstairs and get Nova's push gift. I think she ready for it before she passes out," I told him, handing him his granddaughter.

"You gone spoil that girl to death. Leave me some shit to do," he said, laughing.

I walked out of the room and headed towards the elevator. I pulled out my phone and sent Cru a text that we needed to talk. Getting off the elevator, I made my way through the lobby. I was busy responding to Cru. She must have known it was some shit because she texted back instantly going off.

"Darn, watch where you going?" I heard a female voice say. I looked up from my phone.

"My bad," I said, noticing it was Kelly. The sight of this hoe I wanted to strangle her ass then I looked down at her huge belly. She looked like she was about to pop.

"Well, if it isn't Muza. Nova must've had the baby. You guys still going strong?" she asked.

"Don't sit up here asking me questions like I don't know you and your lil boyfriend robbed me. I swear you lucky you pregnant," I told her.

"So, I assume Nova must've put that in your head. I wonder what else has she told you," she said, shifting all her weight to one side.

"What's that supposed to mean?" I asked. I knew I should've walked off instead of entertaining this chick.

"How well do you really know Nova? You guys were getting engaged until that little shit with Delaunn happened, right. Do you know how she and Delaunn met? Your Nova ain't so sweet. She's an escort," she said. I grabbed her by the arm and pulled her over to a couch that was in the lobby and sat down.

"Come again?" I asked.

"Nova dropped out of college to be an escort. She has had quite a few clients, and they were all rich ranging from politicians, business owners, football players you name it. That's why we always butted heads because I would try to get her to stop but she was addicted to the money. You were her next victim. She bragged about you buying them bags in Burberry that day and instantly came home and researched who you were," Kelly said.

I felt the heat radiating off my back and rising up my neck. This shit all made sense. I done had a baby with a hoe.

"Why should I believe you after the bullshit you done?" I asked her.

"You don't have to believe me, but it's the truth, I'm surprised she

29

hadn't told you yet, but why would she? She got you already, and she had your kid." She laughed.

"Was she still doing that shit when I started coming around and when we got together?" I asked I had to know.

"I don't know," she said standing up.

"It was nice talking to you." She smiled and walked away.

I continued to sit there and digest all that I was told. What in the hell did I get myself involved with? I guess it was true that I really didn't know Nova. I placed my head in my hands and said a prayer because I knew I was about to go upstairs and raise hell. I couldn't go in there without knowing if it was the truth or not, but I was going to ask her first. I didn't even bother going to my car and getting the keys to Nova's push gift. I had upgraded her Range and got her a Bentley Bentayga truck. Nah, she can have the truck. I'm not going to deprive my child because she did just give me the most precious gift.

See, this was the shit that irritated me. I loved Nova's ass to death, but at the same time, I was hating her ass if this shit proved to be true. I walked to my car, retrieved the keys, made my way back inside the hospital, and headed to Nova's room.

Entering the room, Nova was breastfeeding Star. She looked up and smiled.

"I was wondering where you went," she said. I gave her a half smile and scratched my head.

"I had gone downstairs to get your push gift," I said, giving her the box. She took the box and opened it with one hand. Lifting the key, her eyes grew big.

"No, you didn't. A Bentley?" she asked. I nodded my head.

"I ran into somebody downstairs in the lobby," I told her, walking closer to the bed.

"You know Nova while you were giving birth to Star I had made the decision to try and work things out with you. You know you sort of gave me an ultimatum beforehand. I was going to go home call it off with Cru and gives us that chance, but you know relationships should always be built on trust and being honest with your partner, right?" I asked. Nova nodded her head and removed a sleeping Star from her breasts, placing her on her shoulder.

"What are you getting at? I feel you fishing around with this big speech. Who did you run into downstairs?" she asked. I knew she wasn't getting aggravated with me. I was the one that had the right to be pissed and aggravated.

"Kelly," I said, crossing my arms. Nova looked at Uncle Malcolm in fear.

"Baby, I think we need to step out and let Nova and Muza talk," he told my aunt.

"No, y'all stay put. Nova, do you have something you need to tell me or should've been told me before I got your ass pregnant," I fumed.

"Nova, just go ahead and tell him," Malcolm said. I turned to him.

"Oh, so you knew she was turning tricks?" I asked.

"Boy, you better watch your mouth before your ass be down the hall in another room," he said.

"Ms. Elizabeth, can you get her please?" she asked, and my aunt walked over to grab Star.

"So, I take it Kelly told you about my past? And that's exactly what it is. Once again Muza, once you entered my life, I left everything alone, including that part of my life," she said.

"Yeah because you seen me as a come up, researching a nigga and shit!" I yelled.

"First of all, ok yeah when I spotted you in the mall I saw you and was like he's fine and looks like he got money. However, I didn't even know who the hell you were at the time. Even after you asked me in the store that day and paid for my shit after I told your ass no, I could buy my own stuff. I did my research after them damn girls in the store was like *"oh my god! You don't know who that is?"* Who was to say that I ever saw you again? I had no clue when I came to see my mother that I was going to see your ass again. Don't get it twisted. When you needed me to pretend to be your girlfriend and offered to pay me, it wasn't a problem because I needed you to keep my secret also. I couldn't help that I started to catch feelings for you. But for you to stand up there and call me a hoe and regret getting me pregnant is fucked up," she cried.

"I don't want to hear none of that crying because you should've told me. I told you about keeping it real with me when I caught your ass lying to me the first time. How I look being with somebody and you done been on different niggas arms and ain't no telling who you done slept with," I told her.

"Just like you have a past with different women I can't judge you for that, so why should I be judged by something that I use to do? I didn't sleep with every client that I had. This isn't fair Muza. That's all you care about is what the next motherfucker gone say. Everybody in the industry got a damn past, hell it's life," she said. I shook my head.

"Nova, this shit ain't cool. You were a damn prostitute, and you expect me to be like oh ok?" I asked.

"First of all, I wasn't no motherfucking prostitute. I was a damn escort! You slick paid me for services, did you not? You needed me on your arm to portray to the media you had moved on from Cru. You took me to events as your eye candy. It's the same damn thing except you did get some pussy out the deal, which I turned down, but you were like *"we need to get in character it will only help us"* Did you not say that shit? Please tell me how the fuck is it different?" she yelled while clapping her hands. She was pissed now, and that ratchet side was coming out.

"She does have a point," my aunt said. I looked at her like she was crazy.

"Man, y'all tripping. Let this had been Cru's ass and y'all wouldn't be so damn lenient," I said.

"This ain't Cru. This is the mother of your child. The shit is in the past Muzaini. You have a beautiful, healthy daughter here, and she needs both of her parents. How can you say you always wanted a family but run every time some shit displeases you? God forbid you ever get married and do that shit. Everyone has a past, even me. You wouldn't think my ass came out of University Court projects. Grow the hell up Muza," Elizabeth said. Everyone was really acting like I ain't have a right to be mad. I was done with this shit.

"So, you don't have anything to say?" Nova asked.

"Nah, I'm good. I'll be back later," I said, turning to walk out of the room.

"In no way will I ever keep you from your child, but if you leave, I take it as you are giving up on us as in me and you," she said.

"How can you not give me a chance to digest this?" I asked.

"What are you digesting? You either want to be a family or not?" she asked.

I let out a huge sigh and placed my hand on the door opening it. I looked back over my shoulder at all of them staring at me and walked out. I had to leave. The man in me couldn't see the woman I love just parading around with different men. I loved her more than I loved myself, but I wouldn't do nothing but hurt her if I stayed simply because every time I look at her that shit would be in the back of my head. I couldn't give myself fully to Nova just yet.

Novanna

I COULDN'T BELIEVE MUZA, then again, I could this was the typical shit that he did. He was all for self, and he cared what everyone thought regardless of the way it made others feel. Here we had a whole kid together, and he left me. I couldn't control the crying after he left. My father and Elizabeth tried they best to console me.

"Nova, don't even worry about him. You focus on yourself and your child. He will come around. I know him. He just being a man and he's hurt. Give him some time," she said.

"I mean I understand all that, but I told him if he left I was done. He could've stayed and still had the chance to digest whatever it was that he needed to digest. He can go live his happy life with Cru," I cried.

"Ain't shit gone change, and don't you start acting differently because he around. You're my child and you are welcomed in my home. You don't have to want for anything, so that little past life you lived ain't no going back to that. You have made a nice home for you and Star, and your writing is about to take off. I see it. So, stay focus," Malcolm told me. I heard everything he was saying, but was there a prescription for heartbreak because I needed one.

The first night was long for me. I didn't even want to have the baby in the room with me, so I sent her to the nursery. I thought I was going to be able to get some much-needed rest, but that didn't happen. My mind was in overdrive.

* * *

When I woke up the next day, I had paged for the nurse to bring me Star. The door opened and in walked the nurse without my baby.

"Ms. Collier, you were sleeping, and her father is in another room visiting with her," she said. That shit caught me off guard.

"It's time for her feeding so can you tell him he needs to bring her in here please," I told her.

"I sure will," she said as she walked out of the room. Well, at least he came and seen Star. A few minutes later, the door opened, and Muza came in pushing the cot that had Star inside.

"Heyy, mama's baby. You ready to eat?" I said in baby talk as if I didn't see Muza standing there.

I wanted to look at him so bad, but I wasn't about to do it. I reached in and grabbed Star, placed her on my breast, and watched as she ate. She was so beautiful she looked like a mixture of the both of us. He took a seat in the chair while I fed Star.

"I don't want things to be uncomfortable between us whenever I come and visit Star," he said. I didn't even look up.

"Things wouldn't be uncomfortable if you hadn't left how you did. I'm not the one uncomfortable. Like I told you I would never keep you from seeing Star," I told him.

"Nova, you are making this hard being cold and acting as if I'm not sitting here," he said. This nigga was seriously delusional.

"How do you expect me to act? I have to digest all of this. I just had my heart ripped out my damn chest, and you seriously want me to welcome you with open arms. You're crazier and more selfish than I thought," I said. I started to burp Star, and he just continued to sit there looking stupid.

"Things will happen on its own time," I told him.

"I will give you money weekly for her, neither of y'all don't have to worry about anything," he said.

"You are not obligated to take care of me, Star is your responsibility, plus I have more than enough money put up for a rainy day. I'm sure your girlfriend will not like you taking care of the woman you love," I said I hope he caught that because I threw that shit.

"I know I'm not obligated, but what kind of man would I be if I didn't make sure you were straight?" he asked. I was growing tired of this shit.

"Muza, take care of Star, and that's it. Call before you come to my house, and she will not be leaving my presence for the first six months, so if you have any plans where you think she's coming to your house. I suggest you reconsider," I told him, and I was serious.

"Wait why is she not allowed at my house?" he asked.

"You really have to ask? Cru and I do not like each other, ain't no faking the funk at all. You just wait until I get evidence, but I know for a fact that she played a part with Delaunn. I know it, and I feel that shit down in my soul. I do not want that evil wench around my child because one thing you gone find out about me is, I'm not going to play about my child, and I don't mind going to jail," I told him with a serious look on my face.

"I'll respect it for now, but eventually the both of y'all are going to have to get along," he said, which angered me more.

"You say that like you plan on being with her for a long time," I said. Muza shrugged his shoulders.

"I don't know shit to be honest," he said. I didn't even have a comeback. We both sat there in silence. What had we become?

* * *

IT HAD BEEN two weeks since I been home from the hospital. This motherhood thing was whooping my ass. I had started a schedule so that Star and I could get have some teamwork things going on, but she wasn't going, Before the baby, I was a night owl, I did my best work in the wee hours of the morning. But, it seems like Star was taking after me because she would sleep all day and stay up all night. Elizabeth and my father stayed over a few nights so that I could try and get some rest. I couldn't even sleep during the daytime while Star was asleep because I was either taking care of stuff around the house or working on my book.

My child knew exactly what she was doing because she was a damn daddy's girl. One night I was so tired that I couldn't think straight, so I had no choice but to call Muza. I wasn't trying to be disrespectful to his relationship, but a bitch needed help. Nah ok, I really didn't give a damn if I was being disrespectful or not. Fuck Cru. But, don't you know that as soon as her daddy got there, that lil girl went to sleep and slept the whole night. I didn't know what she thought she was doing, but that was not about to become a habit. I ended up hiring a nanny, especially for the daytime, so that I could at least get some rest so that I would be energized for the night in case Star wanted to show out.

Tonight was Ms. Elizabeth birthday dinner, and I asked the nanny to stay over so that I could attend. Star was still too young to be out and about just yet. Looking in the mirror, the baby weight was filling me out just right. My stomach had toned down due to the breastfeed-ing, and my hips and ass were on fat. If I knew one thing, I knew Muza would be there. Searching through my closet, my eyes hit some new Gucci items that I had purchased while pregnant specifically for the snap back. I chose the Gucci stamp print silk shirt, a pair of Fashion Nova high waist ripped jeans and the matching pair of Gucci stamp print pumps. I wore my dreads down in the back and a high bun at the top. I topped it off with some gold accessories, and some Fenty lip gloss blessed my lips. Grabbing my coat, I headed down-stairs to my nanny and Star.

"You look nice," my nanny Maria said.

"Thank you, Maria, I feel nice also. It's been a minute since I have been able to dress up and just get out," I told her.

"Well you have fun, little Star will be perfectly fine," she said, easing my heart.

"If you need anything, just call. I won't be late, and it is plenty breast milk in the fridge," I told Maria.

"Yes ma'am," she said. I grabbed my keys and hopped in my Bentley truck Muza got me and headed to The Hamsteads.

MUZAINI

I stood in the closet tucking my shirt in. I was ready to get the hell out of here. I almost made that shit solo, but Cru's ass wouldn't stop bitching about her going. This was my aunt's birthday, and Cru wanted to feel like part of the family, so she demanded that she come along. Of course, my aunt wasn't having that shit at first, but she gave in and told me to keep her in her place. I walked out of the closet, and Cru was still doing her makeup.

"If you don't want to get left, I suggest you hurry up. I don't know why you are putting on all that shit anyway. You don't need it," I told her. Cru wasn't ugly at all, but she always caked that damn makeup on.

"I'm almost done, goodness!" she yelled from the bathroom.

I grabbed my coat and headed downstairs. A nigga was nervous because I knew that my aunt invited Nova, and I prayed it wouldn't be no shit tonight. This would be Nova and Cru's first time seeing each other since the ball.

"I'm ready!" Cru sang as she made her way down the steps. I shook my head. She was dressed over the top like she was trying to prove a point tonight.

"You like?" she asked doing a twirl.

"Yeah, if we were going dancing or some shit, but we're going to a dinner at my people's house," I said. We didn't have time so fuck it.

"Come on, we already late," I said, opening the door letting her out.

I was silent most of the ride praying to the Lord above let this night be smooth.

"Why are you so quiet?" she asked.

"No reason, just thinking," I said.

"Is your baby mother going to be here?" she asked. I shrugged my shoulders.

"I don't know. Her and my aunt is really cool, so I'm sure she invited her," I said, hoping she would stop there.

"I'm sure she will be there. Who is watching Star though? She should be home with her kid instead of out on the scene," Cru said smartly. Jesus, see I was trying to avoid shit like this.

"First of all, our child isn't your concern, but if you must know, she's taken care of. You are talking about somebody being on the scene girl when we are going to eat and that's it. You act like somebody hitting the club. Don't get here and show your ass. Cru, I swear to God I will turn this car around and drop your ass back off so quick. How you gone speak on somebody's parenting and you ain't got no kids nor do you want any," I said. I knew that hit hard. She crossed her arms and looked forward.

"I can't believe you just literally bit my head off over that bitch!" Cru spat. I slammed on breaks.

"What the hell did I just say? You can get out right here," I told her ass.

"I'm not getting out of shit. I'm your woman, and you will respect me and treat me as such," she said.

"Oh, so now I'm not treating you as such because I spoke up on something that you know nothing about," I said. I started back driving and turned the corner into the subdivision. Pulling into the yard, I got out the car leaving Cru ass sitting there.

Walking into the house, I walked straight in and went straight to the bar. I needed something stiff to drink.

"Well hello to you to, son. Is everything alright?" Malcolm asked. Shaking my head, I let out a huge sigh.

"Man, Cru is gone make me choke the shit out of her. She is always worried about the wrong shit," I said. Unc chuckled.

"You better tell her get her shit together before Elizabeth lets her have it. She already doesn't want her here," Malcolm said. As soon as he said that Cru came waltzing in like ain't shit happen.

"Hey baby," she cooed.

"Where's everybody at?" I asked.

"Sitting in the den waiting on all guests before dinner is served," he said. We all left and headed towards the den.

"Muza, sweetie, it's a pleasure for you to finally join us," my aunt said as we walked in the den. I leaned down and placed a peck on her cheek.

"Hey, Ms. E!" Cru spoke. My aunt gave her a dry look.

"That's Mrs. Hamstead, darling," she said as she took a sip out of her wine glass.

Cru was shocked but laughed it off. I chuckled, took a seat on the other couch, and engaged in conversation with others. Cru took her seat beside me and sat quietly. I knew she had to be uncomfortable, and this was why I told her to stay at home.

"Hey everyone!" I heard Nova's voice. I looked up and my dick started to swell. Nova was looking good and healthy, rocking the fuck out of the Gucci fit she had on, down to the shoes.

"Nova, my baby, you have to show my girls pictures of Star. I've been bragging about her all night," my aunt said. Nova smiled, pulled out her phone, and started showing them photos.

"Chile, if she ain't looking like Muzaini right here. Look Muza," my aunt said. I got up, walked over, and looked.

"I am a fine ass man, so it's only right she took after me," I said cockily.

"Boy, if you don't hush, my child looks like her sexy ass mama," Nova said, pushing me. I laughed.

"Aheem!" I heard Cru clearing her throat. We all turned to look at her like she was crazy.

"Can I see?" she asked. I started to show her the picture and Nova grabbed the phone out of my hand.

"She doesn't need to see nothing pertaining to my child. She will probably try to steal it and sell it to the tabloids or some shit," Nova said.

"Nova," I said, giving her a look like *please don't.*

"Nova, grow up. I have a right to see her. I'm involved with her father and will be around for a long time, and I might even be her stepmother. You can't be childish all your life," Cru said. I felt like shit standing in the middle.

"Childish is my middle name. You don't have any rights pertaining to the child that I pushed out of my pussy. You showed me you can't be trusted, and I can't wait for the day that Muza see your duck ass for who you really are. I'm sure Muza hasn't told you this yet, but I'm going to say this and then I'm going to finish enjoying my night with my family, the one you want so desperately to like you. My child is off limits. If you disrespect my child in any way, I will go to jail proudly and serve my time," Nova said, and she turned to my aunt. "Ms. Elizabeth, I'm sorry I had to go there on your special night. We may continue," she said.

Everyone exited the room, and I stayed behind so that I could have a talk with Cru.

"You just let her talk to me any kind of way, and it's clear that you love her and need to be with her. You won't even ride for me," she cried.

"Are you serious, Cru? Did you not hear the shit that came out of your mouth? Ain't nobody finna let you sit up and talk crazy to them, especially if it concerns their child. Nova had to go through a lot with that shit Delaunn did, and she swears you had something to do with it, so I can't control how she feel about you. You are going to make it hard for a nigga when it comes time for me to keep my child if you keep on with this bullshit. I will drop you before I let that happen. I'm wanting to keep everyone happy. You because you are my woman, and Nova because I have to co-parent with her. I don't need any extra stress," I told Cru. She wiped her eyes.

"But, do you still love her?" she asked. Damn, why did she have to ask me that shit?

"Not like you think I do. I love her for her giving me the greatest gift and that's my daughter," I told the semi-truth. Now if you thought I was about to tell her that I loved Nova more than anything in this world you tripping. I still had to keep my home happy. Cru leaned in and kissed me.

"I'm going to go to the bathroom and freshen up. I'll be back," she said. I nodded my head and watched her walk away.

Why was I playing these games with Cru and myself? No matter how many times I said out loud that I was with Cru, that didn't change the fact that my heart was with Nova. This girl had stolen my heart and was holding it for ransom. I fucked up big time but how was I supposed to see past the betrayal. What she did wasn't minor. She held a whole escort service from me. I'm a jealous ass nigga so to know that Nova had been with many different men in whatever way she was with them, and that bothered the fuck out of me. I kept Cru around because she was something to do and at first, I was doing it to make Nova mad. I wanted nothing more than to be with my family, but I done got myself in some shit.

CRU

*L*ooking in the mirror, I patted dry the tears that were ruining my makeup, fixed my braids, and gave myself the once over. Muza thought I was stupid, but I knew he loved Nova more than the way he portrayed. I don't know why he thought I was born yesterday. No matter how hard I tried, his ass couldn't resist his precious Nova. Then that bitch kept bringing up the Delaunn situation. I wish she let that little shit go. She had to do more than what she was doing to get me to come out of character. I had to remain the innocent look. I had Muza wrapped around my finger.

I exited the bathroom and went and met back up with Muza. Hand in hand, we both, entered the dining room and took our seats. I played my fake ass role and apologized to Ms. Elizabeth, even though I gave zero fucks about her ass.

"Mrs. Hamstead, I'm sorry for any disrespect I may have caused," I told her. She gave me a half smile.

"It's fine, Cru," she said and took a bite of her food.

I was enjoying Nova squirming in her seat as Muza and I got comfortable as if we weren't just arguing earlier. Nova phone buzzed, and she grabbed it. I noticed her cheesing, and I also notice Muza wouldn't take his eyes off her.

43

"Who got you cheesing all hard?" he said. I turned my head so fast towards him, pinching his leg.

"Really, why is it any of your concern what's going on with her phone?" I asked him.

"Girl, stop tripping. I figured it was something with the baby," he answered. I dropped my fork on the plate, making a loud clink and pushed my seat back from the table.

"I'm ready to go. You have disrespected me enough tonight," I said. Nova busted out laughing, and I wanted to jump across the table and beat her ass.

"Muza, take this up out of here. My whole damn dinner has been nothing but drama," his aunt said, pointing at me when she said this. Rolling my eyes, I stormed out of the room. This whole damn family had me all the way fucked up.

I stood outside waiting on Muza who was taking his precious time coming out. All he cares about is Nova and that damn baby. I needed to get into his head and quick. Muza came strolling pass me and hit the lock on the car. I walked to the car and got in not saying shit and I wasn't going to. We drove the whole ride home in silence. Muza hopped out the car all fast and was gone in the house. I slowly walked up the steps and turned the knob to find out the door was locked.

"What the fuck?" I said. I pressed the doorbell and beat on the door.

"Muza, open this fucking door before I cause a scene. You got me fucked up!" I yelled.

He wanted to play these games. I turned around and looked in the yard for a big ass rock. I removed the heels that I had on and walked off the porch, picking up a brick out of the grass. The door opened and Muza stood there filming me.

"I wish the fuck you would with your crazy ass. Take your ass to your house!" he yelled.

"Stop playing, Muza. You can't keep doing me like this," I said, walking up to him.

"Cru, ain't nobody doing shit to you. Your ass is just insecure and

44

making shit out of nothing. You showed you whole ass tonight," Muza fumed.

"I'm sorry. Let me make it up to you," I teased. Muza went back in the house.

"I ain't in the mood, but you can bring your ass in," he said. I followed behind him and walked into the house.

Walking upstairs to the bedroom, I removed my clothes and headed to take me a shower. I laid my phone on the counter and turned on me some music. It just so happen that my girl Cardi B was paused from earlier. I stay in my damn feelings about Muza. I pressed play, got in the shower, and rapped the lyrics to "Be Careful" as if my life depended on it.

The only man, baby, I adore
I gave you everything, what's mine is yours
I want you to live your life of course
But I hope you get what you dying' for
Be careful with me
Do you know what you doing'?
Whose feelings that you're hurting' and bruising'?
You gon' gain the whole world
But is it worth the girl that you're losing'?
Be careful with me
Yeah, it's not a threat, it's a warning'
Be careful with me
Yeah, my heart is like a package with a fragile label on it
Be careful with me

I FELT every ounce of that shit.

"Here you go with the subliminal, indirect, in your feelings shit," Muza said, startling me stepping into the shower.

"Hush, I can't help she is just speaking facts," I said.

"Fuck all that shit you talking and bend over," Muza demanded.

I bit my bottom lip and did as I was told. I felt Muza rub the tip of his dick up and down my slit, and he eased inside of me. I grinded

45

into him while I had one hand on the wall and the other on my leg. If I didn't know any better, I think Muza was trying to punish me because he was beating the fuck out of my pussy.

"Slow down, Muza," I moaned in pleasure and pain.

"Fuck!" he said and pulled out of me. He was irritated and stepped out the shower. Fuck that I wasn't done, nor did I get mine.

"How you go limp like that on me, Muza. That has never happened?" I asked.

"Cru, just forget about it," he said and laid in the bed. I climbed in beside him. I rubbed his back, and he tensed at my touch.

"Baby, what's wrong?" I asked.

"Nothing, I just miss Star," he said, but I knew he was lying. That's when it hit me.

"Baby, why don't you get custody of Star?" I suggested. Muza turned towards me.

"Why the hell would I do that?" he asked.

"I just saying she won't even let you keep her overnight until she's six months. If you had custody, you don't have to deal with that, and you can keep all the money you are dishing out in your pocket," I told him.

"Cru, it ain't like she keeps my child from me period. I can see Star whenever I want to. Why would I bring her here overnight and you don't even like kids, but now all sudden you want to play stepmother of the year? In case you forgot, I'm rich and not hurting for money, so again why would I try and take Star from Nova?" he asked.

"You should just consider it. You're much more capable of taking care of your daughter. Considering Nova's past she shouldn't be raising a daughter," I let slip out.

"How the hell you know about Nova's past because I sure as hell ain't tell you?" Muza asked.

"Huh?" I asked, trying to avoid the question.

"If you can huh you can hear, Cru. How the hell you know about Nova past?" he asked again. I knew I should've shut the hell up.

46

MALCOLM

*E*veryone had left, and I was sitting here enjoying a nice conversation with my daughter.

"I'm shocked you didn't knock that girl head off tonight. You showed a lot of restraint," I told Nova as she sat across beside me with her feet in my lap.

"Man, daddy, she kept on trying me. He should've kept her ass at home knowing good and well nobody here like her ass. I'm so glad I didn't bring Star because I probably would've had to fight her. He was doing her wrong though," Nova said.

As a man, I knew all too well the feeling of juggling two women and having feelings for them both. It was the prime example of Mona Lise and Elizabeth.

"Nova, he's confused as hell and conflicted. He wants to be with you, but he can't put his pride to the side. I told you that this would happen though. But if you ask me, the both of you are going to get back together. It might not be right now, but when the timing is right, it will happen," I said, hopefully easing her mind a little bit.

"Daddy, I admit I went about things wrong with Muza, but I never thought this would become of us or my life. I was playing with niggas just for the money. My goal was securing the bag by any means. I can't help the feelings, and I can't help I got pregnant, I can't even help that I love him. To me, he gave up to easy. I'm sure it's some things in Muza's past that I wouldn't be fond of, but I wouldn't abandon him nor his heart. He was the first guy that I ever loved. I loved him before I loved you. I just hope he realizes it before it's too late," Nova said. I wish I could take her pain away.

"Well, I need to get home to my baby. I missed my little girl," Nova said, placing her feet on the floor and putting on her shoes.

"Give my grandbaby a kiss for me," I told her as I walked her to the door.

"Be careful, and call me when you make it in!" I yelled as Nova walked to the car.

"I will love you!" she said.

"Love you too!" I said as I watched her pull out of the driveway.

Closing the door, I walked back in the house. First thing tomorrow, I was going to talk to Muza and see what the hell was going on.

MUZAINI

I laid awake staring at the ceiling. Sleep was like Nova at the moment, something that I wanted but just couldn't get. When I got in the shower with Cru, I was gone bust this nut quickly and go to sleep. But it's like as soon as she opened her mouth a nigga went limp instantly. I had never had that shit happen to me. I knew exactly what it was. I went in the shower with Nova deep on the brain and so hell the whole time I was hitting Cru, I imagined that it was Nova. Cru just had to open her big ass mouth. But, what was really bothering me was the fact that she brought up something that I know I didn't tell her. Her mentioning Nova's past and how I should take Star away because she shouldn't be raising a daughter made me think about Nova saying Cru was in on that shit with Delaunn. Delaunn knew of Nova past, so how else would she know about that.

I looked over at Cru who just looked like she ain't have a care in the world sleeping peacefully after the night of drama she caused.

49

JON JON

"Her funky ass still ain't answering the damn phone," I said, throwing the phone on the table.

I placed my hands behind my head and closed my eyes growing irritated by the second. The fucking baby was crying and shit. I hopped up and stormed to the bedroom.

"Dammit, Kelly, don't you hear his ass crying?" I yelled.

"Yes Jon Jon, I was getting up," she mumbled.

"Well, you not getting up quick enough. A nigga can't even think with all this hollering," I said, walking over to my son and picking him up. He instantly stopped crying. That little shit touched my heart.

"I know your mama is tripping not doing what she supposed to do. What are we keeping her around for?" I said to my son while Kelly was giving me an evil eye.

It was obvious she ain't like my ass, and the feeling was mutual. I ain't never cared for nobody except my sister and now my son. Kelly came back in the room with a bottle, and I handed him to her so that she could feed him.

"I bet not hear him hollering no more," I told her.

"What did I ever do to you to make you treat me the way you do?

I've always done everything you asked of me, yet you treat me like I'm nothing," Kelly asked me.

I thought about if I wanted to tell her the issues that I dealt with, it wasn't like she was going anywhere. I leaned against the dresser.

"I was only taught to love one woman and one woman only, and that's my sister. She made me who I am today. We met in the foster system, and she was staying with this family that took me in. She protected me from a lot of shit, and we managed to run away from a fucked up situation," I admitted.

"I never even knew you had a sister," Kelly said.

"We barely see each other. She is doing her own thing, and all I know is what she taught me— robbing niggas and whoever for money. We used to set up so many people together. We have been all over in different states and shit. She's got clout like that so finding a mark is nothing," I told Kelly.

I couldn't believe I had told her all that. The only thing I didn't tell her was why I loved my sister. We weren't blood-related, so this girl took my virginity and did things to me a woman should. I loved her differently, and she always told me I bet not ever love another woman. The only thing was she went off and fell in love with another man.

"Well, I'm sorry I'm not your sister, but when I met you, I thought you were something special. I never knew that I was walking into abuse and other things," Kelly mumbled.

I couldn't break now I couldn't let her see me weak. I turned and walked out the room, closing the door. I stood on the outside of the door and closed my eyes.

"I'm sorry," I whispered.

MUZAINI

The next morning, I was out the house and making my rounds. I had a few meetings set up and an interview with 101.1 The Beat radio station. A nigga was drained since I didn't get much sleep, but my job was never done. Walking into my office, I was greeted by my Uncle Malcolm.

"What you doing in here?" I asked, placing my stuff on my desk.

"I went and worked out this morning and decided I needed to come and talk to you about some stuff," he said. I sighed because whenever he needed to talk, it wasn't good.

"I'm sorry about Cru last night," I said, figuring that was what this was about.

"Ain't nobody stutting Cru. I came to talk to you about Nova," he said.

"She ok?" I asked.

"Nova is fine, but we had a talk last night, and this situation between y'all is getting old. I saw a side of Nova last night that I rarely see. That girl loves you with every breath in her body. Now I know it's hard to overlook the escorting thing, but Muzaini, it was a part of her past. Everybody's got one. Stop letting this cruel world dictate your heart because you are really playing with Cru by using her, and God

52

knows if you ever leave her and go back to Nova, she's not gone make it easy for y'all. That girl is evil, and I'm not saying this because Nova is my daughter, but I know she was working with Delaunn," he said. I snapped my fingers, remembering last night.

"You know something last night she was talking mad crazy when we got home and had the nerve to say I should get custody of Star because of Nova's past, and she shouldn't be raising a daughter. I was like how the hell you know about Nova's past, and I ain't never told you. She never answered the damn question," I told my uncle.

"You know you were the first man Nova loved. She flat out told me she loved you before she loved me," he said.

"Damn, Unc I knocked you out your spot?' I joked.

"Shut the hell up. I'm serious. Your family is over there and not over there. Think about that shit and make shit right," he said. He stood up from his chair.

"Let me get my ass home and take a shower. Elizabeth will be blowing my ass in a few," he said, walking out of my office.

"Aite, talk you later, Unc," I said. He threw me a peace sign and walked out the door.

I leaned back in the chair and looked at the picture of Star on my desk. I needed to stop playing and get my family back.

NOVA

J had been writing like crazy since I got up this morning. Star was asleep in her bassinet, so I was getting this word count up. I couldn't wait to release to this book. This was my life story in a way. That's why it was taking me so long to write because I was literally writing as shit happened in my life. After finishing up this chapter that I was working on, I was going to get dressed and head to the mall and grab me some things and pamper myself today. Closing my laptop, I paged Maria, asking her to come up.

"Yes, Ms. Nova?" she asked, entering the room.

"I'm going to hop in the shower and run to the mall. Star is in the bassinet sleeping," I told her.

"I got her," she said, walking over to the bassinet.

I stepped into the bathroom and took care of my hygiene. About forty-five minutes later, I was leaving the house and hopping in my truck. I drove to Green Hills and instantly had a flashback of when I met Muza's fine ass. I smiled at the thought of how far we come. Well, I guess it wasn't nothing to smile about since now we weren't on the best terms. I got out my truck and walked towards the entrance of the mall, and my phone rang. I reached into my bag and grabbed it. Looking at the screen, it was my father.

"Wassup, daddy?" I asked, placing the phone on speaker.

"What you got going on, girl? Where you at?" he asked.

"I just got to Green Hills about to run up a check." I laughed.

"I had a talk with Muza today. I think I might have talked some sense into him," he said.

I rolled my eyes.

"Daddy, you might as well leave that alone. You know he ain't leaving Cruella Deville." I busted out laughing.

I turned the corner and walked into the Louis Vuitton store. I was wrapped up looking at the bags and daddy was going on and on about his convo he had with Muza.

"Hmp, I thought that was you," I heard from behind.

It was a female voice, and I knew exactly who it was. I looked over my shoulder and gave Cru an up and down look. I turned right back around and continued to listen to my father.

"You know I'm still trying to see what it is that Muza saw in you. I thought for sure that when I called Delaunn and told him that we needed to come up with a way to get rid of you, the video would've been enough to send Muza running, but your ass was already pregnant," Cru said.

"You know what you ain't telling me shit I didn't already know. I knew you were in on it all this time. The only thing was getting Muza to see you for the trifling bitch that you are," I told her.

"Don't worry baby girl, I heard the whole thing!" my father yelled. I still had him on speaker phone.

"Well, your little past is going to help Muza get custody of Star. We both feel an escorting whore shouldn't be raising a little girl." She laughed. My mouth dropped.

"Close your mouth, sweetie. I don't have anything for you to put in it," she had the nerve to say. My breathing picked up, and I slowly turned back towards the bags I was looking at.

"It's ok. You should be getting papers soon, bye bye sweetie enjoy your shopping," she said.

I turned around and grabbed her by them long ass braids wrapping them around my hands and flinging her ass on the floor. Once she was down, I climbed on top of her and repeatedly punched Cru in the face. Her bitch ass couldn't fight, but she was scratching the shit out of my face.

"Nova, Nova!" I could hear my father voice yelling through the phone, but I dropped that shit somewhere.

Two employees had run over and tried to pull me off Cru, but my strength was unbearable. Nothing could stop me from continuing to beat this hoe ass. Still holding her hair, I lifted my foot and came down across Cru's face with my Timberland boots. The sight of blood leaking from Cru had turned me the fuck on. I had been waiting for this moment. This bitch had ruined my life.

"Ok, that's enough," I heard the police say, grabbing me and placing my ass in cuffs.

Tears rolled down my face not because I was scared to go to jail, but I started to think of Star. That hoe deserved every damn bit of that ass whooping. I watched as everyone crowded around Cru and they hauled my ass out of the store and into the back of the police car.

MALCOLM

J couldn't believe the shit I was listening to on the phone with Nova. Cru was talking all that shit and Nova done laid into her quick. I placed a call to my friend who worked downtown to see what was going on with Nova. Cru was pressing charges, and Nova was being processed and book. Elizabeth was heading to Nova's to pick up Star, and my ass was trying to get in touch with Muza. The word was that Nova did some hellafied damage to Cru, and Cru was in the hospital. The blows to the face were horrible due to the boots Nova had on. When I got to the precinct and checked on everything Nova was being charged with aggravated assault and other pending charges. Nova's ass didn't have a bond, and this shit was pissing me off. Muza walked in.

"Unc, what the fuck happened?" Muza asked. I shook my head and sighed.

"I've been calling your ass. Cru and Nova got into a fight. The shit was wild. I was on the phone with Nova she was in the mall. She had me on speaker phone, so I heard when Cru approached her, she was saying some crazy shit and taunting Nova about you getting custody of Star. She also admitted that she had planned that shit with Delaunn with that video. I heard that shit crystal clear. I guess Nova snapped and started beating her ass. I'm thinking Nova blacked out and started stomping Cru's head in with her Timberland boots. She is looking at aggravated assault with a deadly weapon. She ain't got no bond, so maybe you can use your clout to see what you can do," I told Muza. Muza placed his hands on top of his head like he was defeated.

"Where is Star?" he asked.

"Elizabeth went and picked her up from Maria," I told him. His phone buzzed, and he looked down and showed me his phone.

"This shit done made *TheShadeRoom*," he said as we watched the attack that someone had recorded.

"Go see what you can do, and I'm going to call up Darius and see if he can take Nova's case and possibly get a bond or some shit," I told him. Muza walked off, and I started calling my lawyer friend.

Muzaini

THESE BASTARDS in the mall wanted to press charges against Nova's ass due to the blood that was left in the store that needed to be cleaned. This shit was sticking, and I needed to get Cru to drop these charges against Nova. My lawyer was going to get the video footage from the store, and I was going to see if I could pay these motherfuckers to drop this shit also. From what Malcolm told me, Cru came in there and started that shit, so maybe I can get them to look at it as self-defense. I was on my way to the hospital now to check on Cru since I was waiting for my lawyer to get back with me.

Walking into the room, a nigga was in shock. Damn Nova. You would've thought that she used a brick instead of a pair of Timberlands and her fist on Cru. Cru turned her head and looked at me. Well, I don't know if she could make out it was me because her eyes were swollen so badly. Cru was looking like Martin when he stepped in the ring with Tommy Hearns.

"It took you long enough," she said.

"In the condition that you're in, you still find time to talk shit. Ain't that what got you into this predicament in the first place?" I asked.

"Correction, your bitch can't take the truth," Cru said.

"And what exactly is the truth? That you walked up to her antagonizing her talking shit. That you admitted to that shit you pulled with Delaunn, or that you lied to her about me getting custody of Star. Ain't nobody finna play with your ass about they kid. You lucky this all you got was an ass whooping. So, what you gone do is drop these charges," I told her, walking up to the bed.

"I ain't dropping shit," she said.

I knew this wasn't gone be easy. My phone started ringing, and I looked down at the unfamiliar number. I stepped out of the room and answered.

"Hello!" I answered.

"You have a collect call from NOVA," the recording stated. I finished listening to the recording and accepted the call.

"Hello!" I said.

"Nigga, you got your motherfucking nerve if you think you about to take my child from me!" Nova yelled into the phone. I looked at the phone.

"Nova, calm down, that shit wasn't true. You're so hotheaded when it comes to Cru. You fell for the shit she was telling you. Now your ass getting charged with aggravated assault with a deadly weapon, Louis Vuitton wants to press charges, so I got to find a way to get this shit to disappear because Cru is adamant about not dropping charges," I told her.

"Deadly weapon? I ain't use no weapon on her lying ass," Nova said.

"Nova, that Timberland that you used to stomp the shit out of her was considered a weapon. You could've caused some damage if you hadn't stopped," I told her.

"Where is my child?" she asked.

"Elizabeth went and got her from Maria, I'll get her once I leave the hospital," I told her.

"It figures you up there with that bitch. You bet not have her around my child. Did my daddy tell you she admitted to that shit with Delaunn? I'm gone press charges against her ass next," Nova said.

"Nova, chill the fuck out. A nigga is tryna get her to drop these charges. I'm trying to get you out and you up here bitching at me. Bye dude," I said, ending the call. Her ass wasn't about to stress me out. I placed my phone back in my pocket and walked back in the room.

"Have you thought about what I said? You owe her Cru because she is talking about pressing charges on you for that video," I told her, hoping she would consider.

"I'm not dropping charges, Muza. Do you love me Muzaini, like for real? Did we ever have any hope of getting to that happy part in our life?" she asked. I thought about my answer.

"Cru, I have feelings for you, but now that the truth has come out about some things that you have done and just over the past couple days you have shown a vindictive side it makes me question your loyalty. You lied to me just like Nova did. I'm not with Nova, so why should I be with you?" I asked her.

"It just feels like that's where you rather be," she whispered.

"Cru, listen and don't take this the wrong way. I was going to marry Nova. Nova gave me something that I always wanted, which was a child and a family. You remember when I use to bring up having a kid with you how you would act like it was the plague or something. You absolutely refused to have a kid no matter how bad I wanted that. At that point, I knew I didn't see a future with you. I was angry when we got back together." I stopped because I needed to be very careful about my next selection of words.

"Things eventually would've got great if you would've stayed in your place, but instead you felt you had to compete with Nova," I said.

"Because I did. I can see the love you have for her. I worked hard within your company and alongside you to deserve the honor of being your wife, not someone that you've only known for a few weeks. How bad do you want me to drop those charges?" she asked.

My ears perked up. Maybe I had gotten through to her.

"What do you want, Cru? I need Nova home so that she can take care of our daughter. She is breastfeeding and shit. Name your price?" I said. I was gone write her ass a check and send her on her way. Cru had an evil grin on her face; at least I think it was a grin. Her face was so fucked up that I couldn't tell.

"I will drop the charges and say that I hit her first whatever you want me to say, only if you be with me," she said.

"Be with you how Cru, ain't we together now?" I asked.

"Don't toy with me, Muza. If you want this to disappear, I will make it happen if you marry me," she said. I started choking and tugging on my ears making sure I heard her right.

"Marry you, Cru, are you for real? This shit ain't no game and marriage isn't something you play with," I said. This hoe was delusional. I was convinced Nova knocked whatever sense she had left out.

"Take it or leave it," she said, crossing her arms.

I needed to think about this shit, and I meant really think about this. I left the room and stood outside of the door. A nigga had to make a few phone calls, especially to my lawyer and look at Nova's options to see if any progress had come along. This shit was starting to get on my damn nerves.

NOVANNA

$\mathcal{W}$hen they called my name and told me I could go, I flew the hell up out that hellhole. That little short period of time let me know that I wouldn't be back. More than anything, I just wanted to see my daughter. I missed her so much. I walked out the gates, and there stood my father and Ms. Elizabeth. I ran over to them and hugged them.

"Girl, you were only locked up for three days," my father said.

"It felt like an eternity. What the hell took y'all so long?" I asked looking into the back seat for my baby.

"Maria has her, and they are waiting for you at home," Ms. Elizabeth said. We got in the car and headed to my house.

"Is all this shit over or is Cru still going through with the charges?" I asked because I know I was looking at a good ass charge.

"It's over. Muza was able to get the tape from the store, and after heavy conversation and some funds exchanged, they backed out because, from the video, you were in there minding your business and Cru came in behind you. As far as Cru, I don't know what Muza did or said, but she backed out also. Luckily Muza's lawyer pulled some strings with the state because even though Cru had dropped the charges, they were going to pick it up and still go through with it," he said.

"He probably had to sell his soul to the devil for her to drop them charges that easy. I'm just glad to be out," I admitted.

"Just stay out of trouble because a lot of money was dished out to make this go away. If you see Cru, don't let her get under your skin," Malcolm told me. I rolled my eyes and looked out the window.

"Did y'all get my truck from the mall?" I asked.

"Yeah, everything is all good. Just go in here and love on your baby because she missed your ass," Malcolm said.

I smiled as we pulled up in my driveway. I exited the car and ran up the steps to my house. Maria met me at the door. I stopped her from handing me Star.

"Oh no, let me shower and get all these jail germs off me, and I'll be ready for her," I told Maria.

"Si," Maria said, and I ran upstairs and removed my clothes hopping in the shower.

While in the shower, I made a mental note to call Muza and thank him for getting me out. I prayed he ain't do nothing stupid for Cru to drop the charges. Stepping out the shower, I threw on some leggings and a t-shirt. I pulled my locs up in a ponytail and headed back downstairs.

"Senorita, I'm making you some steak and shrimp chimichangas, your favorite. Star is in the playpen," Maria said.

"Thank you, Maria," I told her.

I walked over to the playpen, reached down, and picked up Star. I sat down getting comfortable on the couch, and I turned the TV on caught up on my shows I missed while I was gone. Star stirred in my arms. I grabbed my phone and decided to call Muza.

"What's up, Nova? I see your home," he answered.

"Yes, I am. What you up to?" I asked.

"Leaving the hospital with Cru about to head to the crib," he said, I rolled my eyes and sucked my teeth.

"Can you tell her thanks for dropping the charges," I forced out.

"You're welcome, Nova!" I heard her loud and clear.

"Am I on speaker phone?" I asked.

"Yeah!" he said. Muza sounded different like the life that once was in him had been drained.

"Oh well, that's all I wanted," I said.

I really didn't have shit else to say since I was on speaker even though I did want to ask him how he managed to make this happen. But from the happiness in Cru's voice, I could tell it had something to do with the both of them.

"Aite, give Star a kiss for me, I'll try to stop by, and her see her before I leave town," he said.

"Ok, bye," I said, hanging up the phone.

Something wasn't right. I was getting some bad juju from that whole conversation. Maria handed my plate of Chimichangas, I laid Star down and went to work on my plate. I loved Maria cooking. Even though she was the nanny, she went above and beyond when it came to me.

"You ok?" she asked, taking a seat beside me.

"I really don't know. I feel like Muza is keeping something from me. I just got a bad vibe from our conversation," I told her.

"Do you ever think when you finally get the man will everything be worth it?" she asked. I thought about what she said.

"Maria, that is a good question, but now I don't know if I will ever get the man," I admitted.

"Always remember that God don't like ugly, and what's meant to be will be," she said, getting up from the couch.

CRU

"Why didn't you tell her we were getting married?" I asked Muza.

"Because she will find out in due time, and I ain't want to put all that on her today," he said. This nigga thought I was stupid.

"Don't try and play me, Muza. You think because she home that you can renege on this proposal, but I'm ten steps ahead of you. I will have her ass back locked up so fast if you think you are going to get out of this. Invitations have already been sent out, and we are getting married next Saturday," I told him.

I had been planning this wedding for years, so it was nothing to have everything put in place. I was going to get the last laugh.

"Wait how you just gone set a date for a wedding without discussing it with me?" he asked.

"Oh, you thought we were going to be engaged for a few years." I laughed.

"Nah, it's all good, baby. I'll be there waiting on my beautiful bride to walk down the aisle," he said leaning in to kiss me on the cheek.

That's what I thought I had him by the balls. If he wasn't going to tell Cru about the wedding, she would find out as soon as she got her invite in the mail. A small grin eased across my face.

"I can't wait to be Mrs. Muhammad," I said excitedly.

"Hopefully your face healed by then," Muza said I cut my eyes at him because he tried it.

"Don't worry about my face it will be perfect for our wedding day," I said. You just worry about Nova's face when she sees this shit.

JON JON

$\mathcal{I}$ was sitting at the table counting some money from another lick that I had hit. Kelly was in the kitchen fixing a bottle for the baby, and there was a knock at the door. She looked at me, and I looked at her.

"What you looking at? Answer it," I told her.

"I was just making sure because you had all that money sitting out," she said. She walked over to the door and answered.

"Is Jonathan here?" I heard a female voice.

"Who the fuck is it?" I yelled, looking towards the door. Kelly moved out of the way, and my sister was standing there. I stood up

"What you doing here?" I asked. She looked at Kelly up and down, and Kelly did the same.

"Kelly, this is my sister Cru," I told her.

"Oh, nice to meet you. I'll go tend to the baby," she said walking off.

I turned to look at Cru and pushed her back out the door.

"What the fuck you doing popping up over here unannounced?" I asked.

"So that's the little chick you got pregnant. You better not love her. What did I tell you Jonathan?" she asked.

See this is the shit that I was talking about. I was so in love with this woman, and she ain't want me being involved with nobody. To everyone else Cru was my sister, that's how I introduced her, but to me, she was my bitch, and I was her nigga. Been that way since we were teenagers.

"Look, don't be coming over here messing up what I got going on. You out doing you, so I needed help and company. Life gets boring when your gal leaves you for a nigga we were only supposed to hit a lick on," I told her.

"I only came over here to deliver you the news face to face," she said.

"What?" I asked.

"I'm getting married and very soon," she said.

"You marrying that nigga, Cru? Man, you bogus as hell for that," I told her, I felt like my heart was ripped out my chest.

"I'm doing this for us. If I marry him, we won't have to do this shit anymore. What's his is mine, and what's mine is yours. Can't you see that?" she said. I shook my head.

"Nall, what I see is Cru looking out for Cru like she always has. You want to control my life but run yours. I tell you what, you go ahead and marry that nigga, but leave me the fuck alone. You sheisty bitch," I said, turning around to walk back in the house. I slammed the door so hard in her face that my son started crying.

"Everything ok?" Kelly asked. I sat quietly for a minute, and I started to smile because I was gone make Cru pay for this shit. Bitch, you break my heart, and I'm gone break yours.

"I need to tell you the truth about my sister," I told Kelly. She made her way to the couch and sat down beside me. I started to tell her everything, pushing forth with my plans.

MUZAINI

A WEEK LATER

So yeah be mad at a nigga for marrying Cru, but I did what I had to do to get Nova out of jail. I was for real deal dodging her right now. I had been in and out a town, so besides the pictures of Star, I haven't seen her physically. I don't think I could look Nova in her face and tell her that I was marrying Cru. This Saturday was the day, and it is what it is. I walked into my aunt and uncle's house calling out to them.

"Auntie, Unc!" I yelled. I walked into the kitchen, and they both were standing there with somber looks on their face.

"What's wrong with y'all looking like somebody died?" I asked placing my keys on the island.

"That's because somebody is about to die, what the hell is this?" Auntie asked, shoving a card in my face. I grabbed the card and read it, and my jaw started to twitch.

"What you think it is, it's a wedding invitation," I said nonchalantly.

"Oh, no shit we can see that. Why is it a wedding invitation to you and Cru's wedding?" Malcolm asked.

"Because we are getting married Saturday, and I need my family there to support me on this journey," I said.

"You sholl are about to go on a journey to hell, and I will not be there to watch you ride off into the sunset with Lucifer," Auntie said.

"It's funny how Nova said when we picked her up from jail that you probably had to sell your soul to the devil and boom there it is," Malcolm said. Auntie gasped.

"Oh Lord, have you told Nova?" she asked me. I shook my head no.

"Nall, I haven't got around to it yet," I said,

"I wouldn't put it pass, Cru. I bet she mailed Nova an invitation. You better pray she doesn't get an invitation before you have a chance to tell her. When she knock your ass out, don't come back here asking us to fix shit because we are out of it," Auntie said. I knew my auntie was pissed, and a nigga felt bad enough as is.

"So y'all gone be there?" I asked.

"Wearing all black!" she said as she walked out of the kitchen.

"I can't believe you, Muza. What the hell is going on inside that head of yours? This is why I didn't want Nova getting involved with you. I didn't want you hurting my daughter, I didn't think you would, but you have proved me wrong," Unc said, and he left the kitchen also.

I hit the counter in anger and grabbed my keys to leave. I needed to go ahead and tell Nova the news before she found out from someone else.

Novanna

"Ms. Nova, don't cry maybe it's a cruel joke or something. I don't think he would do something like this," Maria said, consoling me. After checking the mail, I end up receiving a motherfucking wedding invitation to Muza and Cru's wedding.

"No, Maria this isn't a joke. That's why his ass ain't been around. He's scared to show his damn face. I knew it was something when I talked to him the day I got out. It was all in his voice that he was hiding something, and it was all in her voice the joy that a woman feels when she happy about something," I cried.

I wonder if my father and Ms. Elizabeth know about this shit and were they keeping it from me. How could he marry her after all the things she has done? I swear something wasn't right about this. The doorbell rang, but I didn't bother moving,

"I'll get the door," Maria said as she left out of my room and headed downstairs. I picked my laptop back up and started to type. Maria came back in

"Who was it?" I asked. She wore an uneasy look.

"It may not be a good idea to have a visitor right now," she said.

"Maria, who is it?" I asked.

Muza popped his head in, and my mood changed instantly. I sat my laptop and got out of the bed.

"What you want?" I asked. I placed my hand on my hips.

"We need to talk," he spoke calmly. I shook my head no.

"I promise you there is nothing to talk about. I just got your little invitation in the mail. I can't believe this shit, Muza!" I yelled, punching him in his chest.

"I'm sorry you had to find out that way, I should've told you sooner," he said.

"You should've told me sooner? Why the hell are you even marrying her? I know you are not feeling her like that. I know you are lying about something, Muza," I told him.

"I'm not lying about anything. I came here to apologize for keeping this from you, but I knew you weren't going to take it well. This will not change our co-parent situation. I will continue to respect your wishes about Star being around her," he said.

"Do you hear yourself? You will respect my wishes about Star being around her. Why in the hell would you even marry someone that your kid can't be around? This shit is backwards as hell. You have no idea how this has hurt me. You are a hypocrite. You called off my engagement because you thought I cheated on you with Delaunn, but here you go and marry the girl who plotted with him. Am I missing something?" I asked I was confused as hell.

"Nova, Cru and I have history," he said. I waved him off because I wasn't trying to hear no more of his whack ass excuses.

"If this has anything to do with her dropping those charges, I will fight my case on my own. I'd rather deal with my own issues than watch you sell your soul to the devil in the white dress," I told him.

"This hasn't nothing to do with that, and that case is closed," he said.

"How come when I pulled it up it said pending investigation?" I asked. Yeah, I had to make sure my name was clear, so something told me to look up case information.

"It shouldn't even be able to pull up. I need to look into that. But please Nova, I will always care about you. I'm here for you and Star," he said.

"No, remember I told you I don't need you for anything. Take care of your child and leave me alone," I told him.

"You're serious right now?" he asked.

"As a heart attack. You can see your way out or go visit with your daughter I have work to do," I said, pointing at my bedroom door.

Muza slowly turned to walk away, and I hated to see him leave because I felt like he was walking out of my life. I wanted to run behind him. I wanted him for myself. I still loved this man, and I couldn't deny that shit if I wanted to.

MUZAINI

*W*hen Nova said her case was pending, that shit caused my antennas to go up. What the hell was up with that shit. I stayed at Nova's and played with Star for about thirty minutes before I left. I couldn't wait to get in the car and call Cru and my lawyer. As soon as I got in the car, I called her ass.

"Hello, my future husband," she cooed in the phone.

"What's up bae, what you doing?" I asked. I didn't want to jump directly into the question just yet. Her crazy ass would've started thinking something.

"Nothing, I just finished up with the caterer," she said.

"Oh, that's what's up. Aye, Darius called me today and said something about Nova's case was pending investigation. What happened, didn't you drop the charges?" I asked.

"Muza, the charges will officially be dropped after we are married. I told you I had my own connections. If this wedding doesn't happen then Nova's ass will be right back in jail picking up where she left off," Cru said.

"Ain't no need for all that. You gone get your wedding, I was just trying to see what he was talking about. A deal is a deal," I said.

"I love you," Cru said.

"I love you too. I'll see you later," I told her and hung up the phone. I dialed Darius' ass next because this nigga had some explaining to do after he done took my money.

"Wassup, Muzaini?" he answered the phone.

"I thought I paid you money to make this situation with Nova disappear for good, especially with them state motherfuckers," I said.

"I did, and then Cru went above the D.A. to whomever she knew up there and told them to hold it for a while. I didn't even know she had clout like that," Darius said.

"What the hell, aye check this out, I need you to draw me up some paperwork, I'm getting married Saturday," I told him.

"Damn nigga, you getting married and this is how I got to find out? What you need some prenup papers?" he asked.

"Nall, I'm going to email you all the details and make sure you send them to Pastor Antonio. I will like to request his services to be our officiant," I told him. There was a slight pause.

"Ok, I gotcha. Send that on through," Darius said.

"I appreciate that," I told him and ended the call.

WEDDING DAY

CRU

I couldn't believe today was my day. The day I was going to marry the man of my dreams. Everyone was giving me such a hard time, but I invested years with this man, so I deserved to be happy. Everything had come together perfectly. We weren't having a huge publicized wedding. We were going to announce to the world on our own time that we had gotten married. That was the thing now in the celebrity world, keeping secrets then boom a baby born or someone got married. Only our family and close friends would be in attendance. Jon Jon was so pissed at me that he hasn't been returning my texts or any of my calls.

Looking in the mirror, I twirled around admiring my Julie Vino dress from the 2018 Venice collection. The sheer and decorative lace that covered the top part of my gown was to die for.

"I can't believe that you are actually about to marry Muza. Is Jon Jon really letting you go through with this?" my ghetto ass cousin Kesha asked. I rolled my eyes. I only invited her ass because her hating didn't work.

"Well believe it. See, you doubted me, but now look at me," I said,

"Yeah, I did doubt you because he had made it clear he didn't want your ass, and I still think you drugged him or something because I can't see to save my soul how you made it happen. Jon Jon ain't came in here shooting up the place either. Yeah, sister, you got the power," Kesha said.

"Jon Jon won't be doing anything. He knows I'm getting married and I told him already," I told her.

"And he ain't trip out on you, Cru? You know how he is about you," she said.

"He hasn't even returned my calls or texts, so I know he is mad, but like I told him, I was looking out for us because he knows whatever I got is his. This marriage will set us for life. Yeah, I know coming into this when I first met Muza was a money scam, but eventually, I grew to love him, and I'm not going to pass up on this opportunity," I told her.

"Well I hope everything works out for you and you don't get a dose of bad Karma," she told me.

"Girl, go take your seat. It's almost time for me to walk out," I told her.

MALCOLM

"*I* don't know why we came to this shit. I feel like I'm betraying my daughter by being here," I looked over and told Elizabeth as we sat out front of the church.

"I don't know why we here either, but we're here, so we are going inside, and as soon as the wedding is over we are heading home. I don't have time to be fake with no damn body," Elizabeth said. I laughed because Elizabeth literally had on all black like she was about to walk up into somebody funeral.

"What's so damn funny?" she asked.

"You dressed in all that damn black," I told her.

"This is just describing my mood. Come on so that we can get this shit over with," Elizabeth said.

For her to be so uppity at times, I loved when the real South Nashville came out of her. I got out the car and walked around to the passenger side and opened the door for Elizabeth. She grabbed my hand, and we walked in the church.

"Do we have to sit in the front?" I asked.

"We are considered his parents since we raised him so yes," she said.

"I thought we walked out with the bridal party?" I asked.

"I don't know, and I'm not walking out with shit. We're about to sit our black asses down right here," Elizabeth said as we took our seats in the front row.

MUZAINI

J ran my hand over my fresh fade and slid my shades on my face. Running my hands down my suit jacket, a nigga was looking spiffy.

"I know you're not about to wear them shades down the aisle, my nigga?" Darius came busting through the door.

"Hell yeah, this is a part of my outfit. What you think I shouldn't wear them?" I asked Darius.

"I mean will your wife think it's acceptable? You know how women are about their wedding day. I could see if we were having an outside wedding, but we are in a church," he said.

"Cru's ass won't give two shits about no damn shades as long as I'm standing there so that she can marry my ass," I told him.

"Have you talked to your baby moms anymore? You sure you are going through with this?" he asked me.

"Nah, not since that day I left her house. I don't want to dwell on that. This is supposed to be my big day, right?" I laughed it off. We shook hands.

"Aite, then let's get this show on the road then," he said as we left the room and headed to the altar.

NOVA

I was parked in the cut watching everyone walk into the church. I even saw when my father and Ms. Elizabeth walked in. Ms. Elizabeth had me cracking up wearing all black, but hell, I guess great mind think alike because my ass was wearing the same thing. I started not to come, and Maria begged me not to, but what I look like turning down the invite. Cru made it her point to rub it in my face that she was marrying Muza by sending me an invitation, so I was gone give sis what she wanted— my motherfucking presence.

I looked at the time, and the wedding should be starting shortly. I opened the door getting out of my truck and made my way across the street and up the stairs of the church. I walked in and took my seat in the very back. I didn't want to be seen.

The music cued, and the wedding started. I could see that Cru planned this shit to the tee. Everything looked nice. I ain't gone hate. Both parties marched in and took their places at the front of the church. I watched Muza as he stood there behind his shades. I chuckled because this nigga knew he was wrong. He did that shit so he that couldn't be read. I could tell he ain't want to do this. It was supposed to be me walking down that aisle heading towards him. The doors reopened, and the music started playing. Everyone stood up as

Cru stood there alone. One of Muza's groomsmen came down and escorted her down the aisle, so I'm assuming she ain't have no daddy. Cru's dress was bad as fuck. I must give it to her ass; she had taste.

Finally, we all took our seats. I noticed my father had seen me because his eyes were glued on me and then Elizabeth turned around also. I smiled and turned my attention back to the wedding. I sat there watching my man, my baby father, the man I loved, standing hand in hand with the devil. My nerves were so torn up that my leg was shaking like a stripper. All I saw were mouths moving. I had tuned out everything so I couldn't hear any words. I had my ears trained to hear what I wanted and needed to hear.

"The bonds this couple has made today are sacred and holy and should not be broken. However, nearly every relationship is tested at one point or another, by conflict, temptation, strife, and change. Will you, their loved ones, family, and friends, agree to help them keep those bonds holy, reminding them of their love for one another, and helping them cross through those stressful periods?" the pastor asked.

"We will!" Everyone in the church answered. I stood up.

"I will not!" I shouted. Everyone turned around in their seats looking at me and whispering. Muza and Cru looked my way.

"Are you really going to do this, Muza?' I asked. My father and Ms. Elizabeth had gotten up and was making their way towards me.

"I don't know what you're doing or why, but this is a huge mistake you're making. You don't love her, and you know it. Your heart is with me and your daughter, and you're willing to walk away from that. Muza, you wearing shades mean you are hiding something. You can't look your bride in the eyes because it ain't me!" I yelled.

"Nova, come on. You're making a fool out of yourself. You don't need no nigga to be with you. I don't care who the hell it is," my father whispered in my ear.

'No, I'm not making a fool of myself. He is being a hypocrite. Come on y'all know that he doesn't need to be marrying her ass, and y'all up there sitting front and center like some happy ass parents.

"You need to leave," Cru said.

"Now you want me to leave, but that didn't stop your messy ass for mailing me an invite. The preacher asked a question, and since we're in church, I told the truth," I responded. Muza removed his shades and looked at me.

"Nova, I have made my decision, and I know you are hurting, but I'm marrying, Cru. Now can you please leave so that we can continue with the wedding?" he asked.

I didn't want it to, but the tears started pouring. I couldn't believe the words that he let pass out of his lips.

"Really Muza?" I cried. My father and Elizabeth were literally dragging my ass out the church. I gave one last look at Muza as he shook his head and turned to finish marrying Cru.

ELIZABETH

*O*oh, child the pain that I knew this girl was going through, I could feel her pain. When Malcolm told me that Nova was sitting in the back of the church, I didn't think she was gone cause a scene like she did. Malcolm and I hopped up so quick so that we could get her out of there. I was in shock. We stood outside the church trying to get her to get herself together.

"Nova, what were you thinking?" I laughed.

"Don't be laughing at that shit. That shit wasn't cute at all. Doing all that damn crying and begging over a nigga," Malcolm huffed.

"Hush, Malcolm! You can't control how she feels about him. I probably would've done the same thing had it been me," I told him.

"That's not how you go about it. Leave that nigga alone, and he will come back," Malcolm said.

"I just wanted to get that off my chest and at least try and give him a chance to make it right. He looked so uncomfortable in there. He doesn't want to marry that girl," I said.

"Well, newsflash he is still in there marrying her ass. Go home to your child and focus on you and her," Malcolm said. I don't know why Malcolm was being such an ass about the situation. I hugged Nova and looked at her.

"You did good. Don't worry about what your father says. We all knew that he was making a mistake, and you're the only one that had the balls to call him out on it," Ms. Elizabeth told me.

I looked back at the church and knew I needed to leave before the ceremony was over because I didn't want to see him. I hugged my father and Ms. Elizabeth again before getting in my truck and pulling off.

MUZAINI

he rest of the ceremony was a blur. My mind wasn't on what was taking place. All I could think about was the hurt on Nova's face and the pain in her voice. I hated to hurt her like that. Cru was looking like a kid on Christmas morning. She fed off Nova's pain.

After the wedding, we had a small reception, and I was drunk off my ass. A nigga got so drunk that I had to leave I was throwing up everywhere.

"Why in the world would you get this drunk and on my wedding day?" Cru asked as she removed my shoes as I laid across the bed. She had been nagging the whole damn time.

"Well, you better sleep this shit off because I will not miss my honeymoon," Cru huffed.

"Wait, how you gone plan a honeymoon without checking my schedules first. I got shit booked for the next two weeks." I sat up, removing my shirt.

"Really Muza, it's our honeymoon?" Cru looked at me in shock.

"I understand that, but you also have to understand we basically had a shotgun wedding. You demanded to be married asap, but you're going to have to wait for the honeymoon because my money comes first. I don't like missing important things. Once this is all over, we can go anywhere you want to go," I told her.

"Anywhere?" she asked. I knew then she was going to plan something outrageous.

"Anywhere," I told her.

Cru jumped up and down and climbed on the bed, and I shook my head telling her to calm down cause a nigga head was spinning. She leaned over and placed a kiss on my lips.

"It feels so good to be Mrs. Muzaini Muhammad," she said. I closed my eyes and smiled but quickly dozed off.

Two weeks later

Things were started to get back on track and spring was approaching, so I was about to debut my Cognac Spring Collection. Over the past two weeks, after the wedding, I had buried myself in my work, and that was really to keep my mind busy and keep me busy and away from Cru. Call me wrong, but it was the truth. I knew that soon Cru's ass would be asking about the honeymoon, so I had to move quickly in what I was trying to do.

I haven't had the chance to see Nova. She was keeping her distance far away from me. When it came to me seeing Star, she had me deal with Maria all the time, or she would try and leave out whenever I came around. I couldn't blame her, but I wish she would at least talk to me. We couldn't go through life like this period. I was going to give her time to calm down, but soon, and I mean real soon, she will sit down and listen to what I have to say.

I pulled up to my lawyer office. He had some news for me that he said he wanted to deliver in person. I was all for it, so I headed there immediately. Walking in to see Darius, I bypassed his secretary and headed straight to his office.

"Wassup man, what you got for me that's so important?" I asked, taking a seat at his desk. Darius turned around and placed some papers on his desk. I picked them up and glanced over them.

"So, this is legit and for real. This shit can't pop back up?" I asked. Darius nodded his head.

"Yep, my brother. It's gone never to be pulled up again, closed all that," he said.

The biggest smile crossed my face, the feeling I was feeling man I couldn't even explain, I jumped up out of the chair.

"What about them other papers I asked you about? You know once I bring it up, I'm gone need proof," I asked him. Darius reached into the drawer and pulled out a set of other papers and handed them to me. Reading over the other papers, I was satisfied.

"Thanks, bro, you really came through," I told him.

"It was nothing. Hit me up though," he said. I placed the papers in my jacket pocket and walked out the office.

NOVANNA

I buttoned up my blouse, grabbed Star, and carried her downstairs. I was running late for an interview. Yes, your girl was applying for a damn job. Don't get me wrong I wasn't hurting for any money, but I wanted to do something that I loved alongside writing books. My book was almost finished, and I was looking to release soon, so in the meantime, I was applying for a writing position for a black newspaper. The paper spotlighted many black businesses such as eateries, hair salons, and anything that was black-owned. My father had put in a good word for me and told me about the place, so I was giving it a shot.

When I got downstairs, I placed Star in her swing and grabbed my laptop and a few mock articles that I had done on some businesses that I had already visited.

"Ok Maria, wish me luck," I told her.

Maria had become a close friend to me, besides Elizabeth. She gave me that motherly instinct that I craved and missed so much from my own mother. I think about my mother all the time, especially when I have my spells of missing Muza. Speaking of him, I have reduced all contact with him. I can't see him because he will see a weak form of me. I know just the sight of him will make me weak. I had unanswered questions, but I wasn't ready to face him to get them answered. He did all his visits through Maria, and I made sure to keep busy so that I wouldn't have to deal with him. From the looks of his social media, yeah, I be creeping, he has down nothing but work and work. He had yet to make a post about him and Cru being married. Cru, on the other hand, hasn't made a marriage post, but she be posting his ass all the time acting like she just the happiest.

"Good luck, Senorita. You will do just fine. Stop and have you a drink to celebrate the good news that you will be getting. I know you will get this position," Maria said. I smiled.

"Thanks, Maria," I said.

I walked over to the swing and kissed Star before heading out. Once in the car, I put the address in my GPS and headed to my destination.

About twenty minutes later, I arrived at my destination. When I looked up at the building, I shook my head. I wanted to cuss my father out. I dialed his number and waited until he answered.

"You get the job, baby girl?" he asked not even saying hello.

"I'm about to pull the hell off. Why you ain't tell me this was Muza's company?" I asked.

"Nova, it's a branch of Muza's company. He doesn't even have anything to do with that side. It's what you wanted. Just go inside please," he stated. I rolled my eyes

"If I see him, I am turning the hell around," I said, hanging up the phone before he could contest.

Opening the car door, I grabbed my things and walked into the building. I looked around, and the place was nice. I couldn't believe this was all Muzaini's. I walked up to the security desk

"Yes, I have an interview on the fourth floor," I told the security.

"Name?" he asked.

"Novanna Collier," I answered. He handed me an electronic key card.

"Take this and go to the fourth floor. Once you get off, this will get you in the door," he said.

"Thank you," I replied headed towards the elevator.

I stepped on the elevator and pressed the button for the fourth floor. I was nervous as hell and praying to the Lord above that I didn't run into Muza. The elevator stopped, and the doors opened. The hallway was empty, so I walked towards the double doors and used the card the security gave me to unlock it. When I stepped through the double doors, my mouth hit the floor. The neon sign that read *Star Editorials* like to take me out. I looked around because this shit had to be a joke. I walked further into the office space and spotted many cubicles that had laptops and all the works. I continued down the hall until I came to a door with a gold plate on it, it read Novanna Muhammad. I opened the door, and Muza was standing against the desk, looking like a slab of ribs.

"Muza, what the hell is all of this?" I asked.

"Is that how you come in an interview?" he asked.

"Muza, I am in no mood for no damn games. What is all this?" I asked again, pointing to everything including the nameplate.

"This is your job. The paper exists, but you got to make that happen. We gone have our own *Flava* magazine going on, but for the black culture. I feel you can do this, take your writing to another level, and put out your dope ass books," he said. I placed my hands on my head and took in everything.

"Wait a minute. What is your wife going to say about all this and why the hell does this plate says Nova Muhammad?" I asked. Muza sat down and pulled me between his legs. I was hesitant, but the cologne he wore was raping my nostrils, and I was falling weak.

"You know and should've known this whole time that I have never stopped loving you. This was all fake. I did what I had to do for her to drop your charges. She was the one that had your case pending to see that I went through with the wedding. She finally had that shit closed, and Darius pulled some strings with the state also to make this shit disappear for good," he said. I hauled off and punched him in the arm.

"Dude, I was at the wedding. You had a whole service, preacher, and everything, so what you mean this shit was fake?" I asked.

"That shit was fake. Well, I knew it was fake. Cru thinks that shit was real. My homie Antonio pretended to be a pastor. He did a good ass job for somebody who only attends church for funerals. Everything was fake down to the marriage certificate," he said. I couldn't believe he did some shit like this.

"Cru is going to kick your ass. Does she know yet?" I asked him.

"Nope, I'm going to tell her. She is waiting on a nigga to go on a honeymoon and shit, but that's why I been prolonging it so that I can get my ducks in a row. I know I'm gone have to get a restraining order against her, and you may have to do the same. But look, I don't care about none of that. This whole time that we've been apart from each other has been nothing but pain for me. A nigga was tired of faking, but I had to do it. I hope that you can see I would do anything for you, I couldn't even have sex with her because a nigga stayed on limp and that shit was getting hella embarrassing. I've wanted nothing more to make you my wife and for us to raise our daughter together. So, Nova will you give me another chance and let's take this new company by storm?" he asked. This was all I wanted, and this shit was finally happening.

"The only way I will accept any of this is when you get all that mess you created with her fixed. I know this shit is going to bring a lot of drama, and I don't want Star around it. So, do what you need to do by getting that shit in order, and then I will marry your fine, black ass," I told him.

Muza smiled and bit that bottom lip. He reached into his pocket and pulled out the same ring that he used to propose the first time, which last time I checked he threw in the trash.

"Umm, I thought you threw that away?" I asked.

"You remember my stylist, Tammara, right. Well, she held on to it. I never knew that when she told me that I would be using it again for you that she was telling the truth. I feel bad for ever doubting us," he said.

"It's ok. Once we get back on track, nobody will ever be able to break us," I told him.

"Let's go have a drink!" he said.

"I guess we can go somewhere and have one drink," I said. Muza lifted me up off the ground and spun me around. I had my man back.

We decided to stop at Bar Louie since it was in the area. I prayed that nobody paid attention to us. We took our seats at a table.

"You want to grab something to eat while we here, or just do the drink?" he asked.

"A drink would be nice. I got to get back to Star," I told him.

"Thank you for doing an amazing job with our daughter. I know you're all headstrong and stayed telling a nigga that you didn't want shit from me, but I was gone take care of your ass regardless," he said.

"Just hardheaded, but I appreciate how even with your hectic schedule that you still make time to be a father," I told him.

"Welcome to Bar Louie. I'll be your server," the waitress said. I looked up and wanted to smack fire from Kelly.

"Hmp, the tables have turned. You back to bussing tables, huh?" I asked. I felt Muza kick me under the table.

KELLY

I had just started my shift at Bar Louie and had picked the section I was going to work tonight. Things for me was slowly, and I mean slowly, getting back to the Kelly I used to be. After Jon Jon confided in me about the truth behind him and his sister, I felt bad for him. He had been practically used, and now he was out for payback. Jon Jon still had issues with being controlling towards me, but at least the hitting has ceased for a moment. He loved our son, and I think that the love he had for Cru was no longer there. Call me stupid for staying, but this was the father of my child. He even paid for me to get back in school so that I could finish out my last year.

I grabbed the menus and walked over to the table.

"Welcome to Bar Louie, I'll be your server tonight," I said. When the couple looked up, I was looking at Nova and Muza. I could've sworn he was married to Cru.

"Hmm, looks like you back to bussing tables," Nova said.

I knew her ass was gone say something slick out the mouth. That's just how she was built, and I knew I deserved all the backlash. I could tell Muza kicked her under the table because she looked at him right crazy.

"I can get you guys another server if you would like," I said. Muza spoke up

"No, it's fine. We're just getting drinks anyway," he said. I leaned down and pretended to show them the menu because I knew my boss was looking at me, so I had to look busy.

"I really need to talk to you guys, but my boss is a bitch, it's something that I know you would want to know about your wife," I told Muza. He looked at me with a side eye.

"I know the owner. Tell him you're taking a ten-minute break and that I requested it," he told me. I stood up from the table and walked off to find my boss.

Mr. Perkins, Mr. Muhammad is in my section, and he has requested that I take a ten-minute break so that we can discuss some business," I told my boss, pointing to the section. He looked over my shoulder to makes sure I was telling the truth.

"Go ahead," he said.

I turned around and walked back to the table where Nova and Muza were sitting. I stood there, and Muza cleared his throat looking at Nova. She sucked her teeth and scooted over so that I could sit down beside her.

"So, what do you need to tell me about my wife?" Muza asked.

"Sometime before the wedding, Jon Jon had told me he had a foster sister. He left it at that because I had never known he had a sister. So, one day his sister decided to visit, and when I opened the door, it was none other than Cru. She was rude as shit, so they stepped outside. When Jon Jon came back in he was pissed about her getting married, and I found that weird. That's when he said he needed to tell me the whole truth about Cru. Jon Jon would tell everyone that he and Cru were brother and sister because they were foster wise, but it got to a point where they ran away and started messing around with each other on a romantic level. He was in love with Cru, and she was in love with him.

They started hitting licks on folks, and that was their way of making money. Jon Jon said they hit many different states. When she first met you, that's what you were. She told Jon Jon that by marrying you, he was going to benefit also. Jon Jon wasn't trying to hear that though. I don't know what type of hold she had on him, but that nigga ain't been right since," I told Muza. Muza's whole demeanor changed, and he looked like he was ready to kill somebody.

"Why the hell should he believe you after all the bullshit you did? This is right up your alley being messy as hell," Nova said.

"I understand what you're saying, but I don't know what made me do the things I did, but I'm starting to get my life back on track, and when I told you guys that Jon Jon was hurt about this, I meant that shit. He wanted me to tell somebody. This nigga wants Cru to hurt like she hurt him," I told Nova.

"Thanks for telling me this, but this doesn't make up for the shit that you and your lil boyfriend have done. Y'all some fucked up individuals, and he's really fucked up. But, you guys should remember that Karma lays ahead somewhere, so I don't even have to lift a finger," Muza said.

He stood up from the table and looked at Nova. Nova looked at me, and I slid out of the seat and let her get up. They started to walk off, and I called out to Nova.

"Nova, I hope you finally get the happiness you deserve and congrats on your baby," I told her.

I felt like that was going to be my last time seeing her and I genuinely was sorry for everything I did. I hated that I messed up our friendship for Jon Jon.

"Take care Kelly," she said then her and Muza left.

MUZAINI

I really wasn't expecting Kelly to tell me that shit she told me. I wanted to roll up on Cru and have Nova whoop her ass again, but I wasn't tripping at all because I was gone have the last laugh anyway. I walked Nova to her car, and we stood there in silence.

"So much for our drink," I said. Shaking her head, she looked at me.

"It wasn't meant to be. I mean in a way it was because we wouldn't have come here if it wasn't, but good thing we did. I can't believe this shit though. Like this whole time, they've been playing. What you gone do?" Nova asked.

"I'm gone go home like ain't shit happened, then just tell her ass about Jon Jon first, then I'll spring the shit on her about the wedding last," I told her.

"Well, be careful, and I'm a phone call away, so if you need me to come through, you better hit me." She laughed.

"Oh, Mayweather, I know your ass gone come off the wam," I said, causing us both to bust out laughing. I leaned in and kissed Nova.

"I love you, girl," I told her.

"I've always loved you," she said. I opened the truck door for her and helped her inside. I watched as she pulled off.

Walking to my car, I ran down what I was going to say so that I hit everything on the head when I confronted her about this shit. This bitch has been a shyster all her life. That explains the no parents or the past she barely talked about. Cru put on this front like she came from money, but it was really another nigga's money. This bitch wasn't gone see a red cent from me ever again. I started up my car and drove home.

During the drive to my crib, all I could think about was finally be able to start my life with Nova and my beautiful daughter. See, Cru outsmarted me once, but what I was about to tell her I know for sure will be the get back that she deserved. I didn't find no wrong in what I did. Look at all the shit she did to me. She's been playing me the entire time. I hit the steering wheel because the more I thought about it, the more I found myself seething.

I pulled into the driveway, making sure not to block Cru car in because she was leaving tonight. Getting out, I stormed into the house. When I entered the house, the lights were dim, and there were candles lit everywhere. I rolled my eyes at the slow music playing in the background. When I walked into the kitchen, I ain't gone front. Cru was standing there in a nice little lingerie piece.

"Hey, my love," she said in her sexy little voice. I flicked on the lights and started blowing the candles out.

"What you doing trying to set the place on fire then collect some insurance money off of me?" I asked.

"No, I was trying to set the mood and be romantic with my husband. Why you come in here messing up shit?" she asked.

I sat down and pulled out my phone and the paperwork I had gotten earlier from Darius.

"I need to plan this honeymoon," I said. Cru pulled up a chair.

"About time, where we going?" she asked. I laughed and looked at her.

"We are not going anywhere. This is for Nova and me," I said nonchalantly. Cru stood up

"Excuse me, what the fuck is going on?" she asked with her neck rolling and in her pure ratchet form.

"That's the Cru I was waiting to talk to. That's that foster child, set niggas up Cru, ain't it?" I asked. Cru started fidgeting.

"What are you talking about, Muza?" she asked still playing dumb.

'You know exactly what I'm talking about. Your brother /lover Jon Jon ratted you out. So, this whole time you really been playing a nigga," I said.

"No, I don't know what you are talking about. I love you Muza," she said, walking towards me.

"Don't come over here. Why the fuck you keep on lying, Cru? Your time is up, and I know everything. I even know about your most recent visit to him and the conversation y'all had. You told him you were gone be set once you married me and for him not to be mad. I was a lick to you at first, and I guess that's why he robbed me awhile back. You sent that nigga here along with Kelly," I said.

"Who the fuck is Kelly?" she asked.

"Don't worry about all that. Your time is up," I told her.

"My time is up? You can't get rid of me that easy. Did you forget we are married? I will take you for everything," she really had the nerve to say. I couldn't contain my laughter.

"Did you ever think about why I didn't get you to sign a prenup? Did you really think I loved you that much to just up and marry you without securing my money?" I asked. The look of fear on Cru face was priceless.

"What the hell are you trying to say?" she asked.

"We are not married, my girl. You really thought I would marry you after all that shit happen. Girl, that didn't make no type of sense. My homie Antonio, I paid that nigga to be the preacher. He wasn't no real pastor. The wedding certificate we signed wasn't real, I had my homie scan and make up some shit. Girl, you thought you played me, but you were getting hella played," I told her. Cru came towards me swinging

"You petty son of a bitch!" she yelled. I grabbed her by her hands.

"As much as I want to beat your ass right now, I am not a woman beater, but your ass is getting dragged out of here today," I told her, pulling her ass towards the door. She was kicking and screaming, and I kept on pulling until I got her on the porch.

"Muza, you can't do this!" she yelled. I looked down at her and turned to walk back in.

I grabbed her keys and her bag off the door side table and walked back outside where she was standing and trying to make her way back in the house.

"Cru, don't make me call the police on you. Take your shit and get the fuck off my property. I bet not see you back on my property or better yet around me period!" I yelled. Slamming the door, I locked it and walked into the kitchen to fix me a drink.

CRU

I stood there on the porch still trying to process what had happened. How the hell did this happen? I wasn't really married to this man? All these questions started to torment me. I slowly picked up my keys and purse and walked to my car still dressed in the lingerie that I had put on. I couldn't believe he threw me out like that. My mind instantly went to Jon Jon, and I got livid. I couldn't believe that he would do this to me. I reached in my purse, got my keys out, and hopped into my car. Starting the car, I looked at Muza's house one last time before pulling off.

It wasn't like I didn't have nothing because I had made a pretty good living off licks and saving money, but I didn't want to go back to that life. That wasn't who I was anymore, and I had to go see why in the hell Jon Jon did what he did.

Pulling up to his place, I parked my car and got out walking up to the door, I didn't care what the hell I looked like and his bitch better not say shit to me. With my hand formed in a fist, I beat on the door like I was the damn police.

"Jon Jon, open this damn door!" I yelled. I heard the door unlock.

"Bitch, what the fuck are you doing here?" Jon Jon asked with a mug on his face.

"Why did you tell Muza all that bullshit?" I asked.

"You walk around here like a nigga ain't got no feelings all the shit I did for you. Bitch, you're just as scandalous as any other bitch out here. Now that you done got found out, you want to come back here questioning me. Hurt people hurt people, right?" he had the audacity to say. I launched towards him trying to fight.

"Man, get your ass off me, and I ain't the one that told your little dude anyways," he said.

"Well, if you didn't tell him, how the hell does he know everything?" I asked.

"Oh, I told my girl. I guess she ran into them. You know she used to be cool with Nova," he said, crossing his arms.

"So, you let that little bitch come and just mess up what we had?" I asked. Jon Jon started laughing.

"Mess up what we had? Cru, you messed up what we had when you fell in love with a lick then tried to push me away like I wasn't shit. I got a kid now, so I don't need your type of negativity around me," he said. To know that he no longer cared bothered me.

"I hate you, Jon Jon!" I yelled, and I smacked his ass with all my might. Jon Jon grabbed me around my neck, and I didn't see that shit coming.

"You of all people should know to keep your hands to your damn self," he said through gritted teeth as his grip got tighter.

"Jon Jon, let her go!" I heard the girl that was holding a baby come in behind him.

"Nah, fuck that. She wants to come in here and put her hands on a motherfucker. I done hurt people for way less," he told the girl.

I had scratched up his arms trying to get his hand from around my neck, but his strength was unbearable. I felt myself getting weak, and I could no longer put up the fight.

"Jon Jon, she is turning blue. Oh my god, let her go!" she screamed.

KELLY

$\mathcal{I}$ was in the room trying to put my son to sleep. I was tired as hell. I had literally just got off work. It hadn't even been ten minutes, and I was still in my work clothes. The loud beating at the door startled me at first, but when I heard a female yelling Jon Jon's name, I knew then that it was Cru. Word must've gotten back to her about what had happened.

I smirked a little. All I heard was her and Jon Jon going back and forth in the living room. I wasn't going to step out, but when I heard her hitting him, I decided to look. Jon Jon was choking the shit out the girl, and I can't say I was surprised. That nigga was crazy and didn't give a shit. I know, my ass has been beaten plenty of times by the hands of that nigga. It was started to look ugly, so I had called out to him to stop, but he was in a trance, and he wasn't trying to hear nothing I had to say. I could tell Cru was getting weak because she had stopped fighting. Her strength was becoming weak. I had to do something and something fast because Jon Jon was on the verge of killing this girl. I walked out of the room and placed my son in the car seat.

"Mommy will be right back," I told him even though I knew he didn't understand shit I was saying.

Walking back into the room, Jon Jon was still choking Cru, and she looked to be lifeless. I looked around, grabbed the statue off the shelf, and hit Jon Jon over the back of the head, causing him to drop Cru and fall beside her.

"Shit!" I whispered and ran to Cru's side and checked her pulse. There was nothing, and she laid there lifeless. I looked over at Jon Jon, and he was out cold. He was still breathing. I was not about to go down for any of this. I grabbed my cell phone and called the police.

"Yes, there has been an incident at my home, and I need the police here right away. I think one person is dead," I told the operator.

"Ma'am, can you tell us what happened?" the operator asked.

"I came home from work, and my boyfriend was arguing with his ex-girlfriend. Things got heated, and he started choking her and never stopped. I hit him over the head to break them a loose. He's still breathing, but she has no pulse," I told the operator.

"Ok, ma'am stay put. Someone should be pulling up shortly," the operator said.

Hanging up the phone, I just prayed that Jon Jon didn't wake up. I took that chance to go in the bedroom and clean out every red cent he had in the damn safe. He was always so damn mean that I made sure to watch everything he did and paid plenty attention when he didn't think I was. I placed all the money in a few duffle bags and a baby bag. Once the police came to get his ass, I was going to make a run for it.

After packing the bags, I walked back into the living room and made my way to the door that was still slightly ajar from when they came in the house. I heard the sirens outside, so I opened the door wide and waited for the cops to enter.

The cops came in and started processing the shit, and sure enough, Cru was dead. This man had really killed her. About time the officers got to Jon Jon, he was stirring and coming to after being knocked the hell out. When he noticed Cru laid out, this nigga started going crazy and crying.

"Oh my god, what did I do?" he cried. He looked at me, and I shook my head.

"I'm sorry Kelly, please do right by my son," he said.

This nigga was ugly crying, and I ain't ever seen no supposed to be hard ass nigga break down like this. I knew he had blacked out when it came to him choking Cru, and that's why I did what I did. He loved Cru, but he was just a man scorn.

When they placed him in the back of the police car, he looked so pitiful, especially when they brought Cru out in the body bag. The police remained at the scene for what felt like forever. No soon as they left, I grabbed my bags and all the money and placed my son in the car and we were getting the fuck out of Nashville for a while. I would just have to finish school somewhere else. My time here was done.

Novanna

MY ASS WAS happy and in a good place since Muza left here earlier, and I was writing my ass off. I was literally about to finish up this book and send it off for editing. I was waiting to hear back from Muza too, and his ass still hadn't called. I know one thing his ass bet not be over their kissing Cru's ass. There was a knock on my bedroom door.

"Come in!" I yelled. Maria walked in with a frightened look on her face.

"What's up, Maria?" I asked.

'Do you know the name of the young woman that Mr. Muhammad married?" she asked, which I wasn't expecting.

"Cru, what about her?" I asked.

"Do you know her real name? she asked, reaching for the remote to my TV.

"No, what girl you are scaring me," I said, looking at the TV Maria had turned it on News Channel 5 it was a breaking news story. The headline read: *1 dead and 1 arrested*

"Turn it up!" I yelled at Maria, causing her to jump.

"We are on the scene of a murder, details are still being handled. We don't know the motive behind this, but one man has been taken into

custody," the reporter said. My heart started racing. Oh Lord, what did Muza do?

"Arrested was Jonathan Boyd, he has been taking to the jail. The victim was Crumari Noble. We are unaware of what took place, but officers said Ms. Noble appeared to be strangled and that it was a scuffle involved. We will have more details later as we get them in," she said, and the news went to a commercial.

I sat there with a blank stare. I couldn't move I couldn't do nothing.

"Nova, you need to call Mr. Muhammad. This is serious," Maria said, giving me a shake. I shook my head.

"I'm sorry. This is just so crazy. Oh Lord, yes I need to call Muza," I said, grabbing my phone and calling him.

The phone just rang and rang, and I was starting to get worried. I jumped out of bed and threw my sweats on. My phone rang, and I jumped to answer it.

"Hello, Muza?" I asked.

"No, this is your daddy. Did you see the news?" he asked.

"Yes, daddy I did, and I'm trying to get in contact with Muza. This shit is crazy. He was supposed to tell her about us and this fake wedding shit," I said.

"What fake wedding shit?" he asked. I didn't have time to go into details right now.

"Daddy, I promise I will tell you everything. Let me call Muza again," I told him

"Ok, baby girl," he said. As soon as I hung up, I dialed Muza again, this time he picked up.

"Hello," he answered groggily.

"Muza, where the hell you at?" I asked.

"I'm at the crib. A nigga got on that drink and passed out," he said. I rolled my eyes.

"So, I assume you don't know what happened tonight?" I asked.

"No, what's up?" he asked.

"Crumari aka Cru is dead, your boy Jon Jon killed her ass, and that shit all on the news," I told him.

"You are kidding, right?" he asked.

"Hell no, did you ever talk to her?" I asked, wondering if he told her the news.

"Yeah, I dragged her ass out of here and told her she better stay away from me. I told her about that Jon Jon shit, and that's probably why she was over there trying to confront that crazy ass nigga. Damn, that's fucked up. Cru did some fucked up shit and hell I wanted to beat her ass, but I would never want no shit like this to happen. Did they say how she died?" he asked.

"They said she appeared to be strangled. Look, I'm going to pack Star and me a bag, and we are coming over to stay the night with you," I told him.

"Nah, it's too late to bring her out. Let me make some calls first then I'll come to your crib," Muza said.

"Ok, be careful. Love you," I told him.

"Love you too," he said.

I took that time to call my father back and fill him in on everything that had transpired. Apparently, he was out of the loop.

"What's up, baby girl? Did you get in touch with Muza?" he asked.

"Yes, his ass was knocked out drunk. He's on his way to stay the night with Star and me," I told him.

"Y'all couldn't wait for that girl to die so that y'all could be together, huh?" he asked me. I didn't want to laugh, but I swear sometimes this man had no filter.

"Daddy no, don't say that. I may not have liked the girl, but I don't wish death on no one. So, I take it you knew all about this fake ass interview with Muza, right?" I asked.

"I didn't know the details. He just asked me to get you there, so I had a part in that. Why what he do?" Malcolm inquired.

"Daddy, this man gave me a whole floor for a business to run. It's called Star Editorials. He wants me to do a magazine or paper something like that show *Living Single* where she had that magazine *FLAVA*, do you remember?" I asked.

"Yeah, boy that nigga got moves. His little slick ass." Malcolm laughed.

"Yeah, he's slick alright. So, I walked into the office and saw my name on the door, peep this it said, Nova Muhammad. I'm like what the hell is going on? This nigga tells me that his marriage to Cru was fake down to the preacher and the marriage certificate. The only reason he married her was so she would drop the charges on my case." I sighed, letting out relief as I thought about everything.

"Well damn, I knew it had to be something as to why he was marrying that girl. Well, thank God it was fake. I guess I got to apologize for calling him a dumb ass nigga," Malcolm said.

"Daddy!" I laughed.

"What? That was the dumbest shit ever. I was like this boy done threw his life away. Well, I'm glad that things will finally be good for y'all," Malcolm said.

"Yeah, I hope that we can move forward, and it's been a long time coming. I just want to be a wife, publish this book, and run this company. I'm claiming it now," I told my father with a smile on my face. The door to my bedroom opened, and Muza walked in.

"Hey daddy, I got to go. My man is home," I said excitedly.

"Bye girl," he said. I placed the phone on the night table and watched as Muza came and sat at the edge of the bed.

"You ok?" I asked him. I knew he probably was harboring a lot.

"Yeah, it's a lot to process. You know it's death, and I've never been the one to process death well. I don't know how this may sit with you, and I don't want to start our relationship back with keeping things away from you or just starting out on the wrong foot period, but I need to pay for her funeral arrangements. It's only right. The media is about to eat this shit up. I have to make a press release somewhat about her past but also not giving up too many details," he told me. I lifted the covers and crawled over to where he sat, placing my arms around his neck.

"I'm gone be here every step of the way, and we will get through this together," I told him, placing a kiss on his lips.

MUZAINI

*W*hen I rolled over, seeing Nova knocked out with Star on her chest, it made a nigga feel like a king. This was all I ever wanted. Damn, who would've thought Nova and I would even get here. I hated the way I treated her after finding out about her past, but that was something that I promised I would never bring up. I wanted to uplift my woman and give her everything she needed to prosper and follow her dreams. I wasn't going to be that nigga that kept reminding her of all that I did for her. We were gone get this money together. Star Editorials was hers, and I trusted she would give it the love that it needed to grow into the next big thing.

I agreed to do one interview today addressing the situation with Cru, and I wasn't gone speak on it again. I was waiting on Darius to get back with me. He had gone and spoke with Jon Jon. I just wanted to hear his side of everything so that I could know exactly what happened. Knowing Darius' ass, he'd probably come from down there and be this nigga lawyer. That nigga was all about a dollar, but shit, I don't blame him.

I eased out of bed and headed to the bathroom to handle my hygiene. I stepped into the shower and turned the shower on letting the water just run over my head. I know I didn't move for about ten minutes. The last two days had my mind on overload. It was like being on a high and not being able to come down. I was tired of being high.

"So, you thought you were gone be able to get naked around me and I not do nothing?" I heard Nova's voice.

I looked up, and she stood outside the shower, pulling her t-shirt over her head. My dick instantly started rising. Man, a nigga ain't felt the inside of Nova body in so long, shit. I opened the door, and she stepped in.

"Girl, your ass was gone get this dick sooner or later. I didn't want to wake Star," I told her. I moved one of her locs out of her face and kissed the tip of her nose.

"Where she at anyway?" I asked.

"Still sleeping. I put her in her bed and turned the monitor on," she said, pointing to the sink where the baby monitor was sitting.

"Oh well in that case," I said, dropping down to my knees.

I pushed Nova on the wall in the back of the shower. Before I devoured her, I just looked at my pussy. Yes, this was mine and was gone forever be mine. That shit was pretty and fat. Nova was tantalizing. Shit, just being in her presence I was ready to eat her ass like a biscuit. I placed my tongue on her center and sucked out her soul. Nova had one hand on the wall, and the other was on top of my head, burying me further in her pussy.

"Shit, Muza!" she moaned.

"You miss this?" I asked because God knows I missed every inch of her.

"Yes," she answered.

I stopped licking and turned her around. I grabbed the both of her hands and placed them on the wall like I was the police and was about to frisk her ass. I found my way to her ass and gave her a deep licking. All I wanted to do was please Nova in the worse way. This felt like I had to prove myself all over again. It's been so long since we've been intimate. I was ready to feel inside now, grabbing her hands

"Touch the floor," I demanded.

Nova bent all the way over and touched the shower floor. I massaged her clit before easing inside of her. *Lord, don't let a nigga bust in three seconds,* I thought. Nova's shit was tight as fuck. I started out with slow easy thrusts so that I wouldn't hurt her.

"Muza, you know how to fuck me, and I need you to do that," she had the nerve to say.

Well damn, a nigga was trying to be gentle and shit, but if it was the dick she wanted, I was gone give it to her. I started beating the shit out of her pussy. Nova was a freak, and she took the dick well. She was matching my thrusts by throwing that ass back and bouncing on the dick while bent over.

I smacked her on the ass as I continued to slide in and out of her pussy. A nigga didn't know how much longer I could go because she was about to feel a nigga's nut. I slowed down and pulled out, and Nova turned around and got on her knees, taking me in her mouth. I couldn't do shit but throw my head back because Nova had that damn tornado mouth. Her head game was stupid, and she had a nigga's knees weak. I wanted to grab her hair, but I had to hold on to something. You know what made that shit ten times better. She never took her eyes off me when she sucked. She wanted to look me dead in my eyes and see that she took my soul because that's exactly what she was doing. Using her hand to jack me off and that vacuum mouth of hers, I was nutting in seconds. Nova smiled as she continued to suck, and I wanted to pop her ass on top of her head. She sucked a nigga dry and swallowed my kids.

"Damn, girl," I huffed, trying to regain my composure.

Nova smiled and wiped her mouth. Grabbing the soap, she started to wash off her body. Just looking at her body, I wanted to go another round, but I had to get the hell out of here. I followed suit and washed my body also before getting out the shower.

While getting dressed, my cell rang. Looking at the screen, it was Darius.

"Wassup, nigga? It took you long enough," I answered.

"Man that shit was depressing as hell. That boy for real deal snapped all because he loved her, and she played him. I've never seen no dude stressed about no gal like that. Shit, all we do is move on to another one. But considering their history, and how they only had each other while they were in the foster system, Cru was all he knew. I wish the shit would've come out that y'all wasn't really married first before he fucked his life up over that girl. He got a whole son out here that may never see his ass again, and they said old girl left town immediately," Darius said, filling me in.

"I see where you are coming from, but Cru had issues. Her issues were beyond the shit that happened to her. She put that man through all that shit feeding into his head that she was his and they were gone be together and live off my money, and he snapped," I told Darius.

"He just kept apologizing and shit. I hope he doesn't do nothing to hurt himself while he up in there," Darius said.

"He'll be aite. Let me get my ass dressed and get to the office because this camera crew will be there for the interview," I told Darius.

'Aite man, keep yo head up," he said. Hanging up the phone, I started to get dressed.

"You want me to go with you?" Nova asked as she came into the room.

"If you want to. I'm just going to the office," I told her.

"I'll let you handle that, but I am going to my office so that I can get things running. I'm eager to get this off the ground," she said. We both continued to get dressed and got ready to go our separate ways.

ARRIVING at the office once Nova got off on her floor, I kissed her and continued up to my floor. The news crew was already there and waiting.

"Thank you guys for being patient with me this morning. I had a hard time getting here," I said, fixing my jacket.

"No problem, we are just thankful that you are giving us and only us this interview. I'm Lacy Taylor, and I will be conducting the interview," she said. Thank God they sent a sister maybe she will have some sympathy for a brother.

"Have a seat," I told her. Lacy sat down. Her camera crew was working the room.

"They're just going to start setting up, and we can have an off the record conversation.

"Ok, that's fine," I told her.

"Anything you want us to know off the record that I may ask during the interview that you don't want anyone to know?" she asked. I knew I shouldn't tell this lady, but maybe it would get her to see where I was coming from.

"Well, everyone knows that Cru and I had history and that she was in the spotlight with me. Eventually, we did break up, and some things came about that I never knew Cru was behind. I was going to get engaged to the woman I'm with now, but Cru was behind some things that stopped that. She and the woman I'm marrying had got into a big fight, and I sort of told Cru I would do anything if she dropped the charges. Cru asked us to get married, so we had a ceremony and all that, but it was private. Once the charges were dropped, I told her that the marriage was fake, as well as the pastor and the certificate. So, if you can avoid that or similar questioning that would be perfect. I'd just rather say we broke up," I told her. Lacy was stunned. I could tell by the look on her face.

"Wow, so you really had a fake wedding? Who thinks to do something like that?" she asked me. I smiled.

"You would do just about anything to protect the one you love, "I told her. A mic was placed on my suit jacket, and the lighting was turned on.

"Ok, so I'm just gone to ask you a little bit about your background. You can tell what you want us to know about you and Cru and anything you know about what took place last night. You ready?" she asked.

"Yep," I said. I watched as the man counted down on his fingers, and we were live.

"Hi, Lacy Taylor here and I'm sitting with the one and only Muzaini Muhammad with an exclusive interview that you will only hear from us about the late Crumari Noble. How are you doing, Mr. Muhammad?" she asked.

"I'm doing ok, considering the circumstances," I said.

"I'd just like to say that we are sorry for your loss. Can you give us a little background about you and Crumari?" she asked.

"Sure. Well, I met Cru about four years ago, and we instantly clicked. Our relationship was up and down, but that's normal now. I always spoke on wanting a family, and that was something that she just didn't want. I never knew the history of why she didn't want kids, and I later found out that she was a foster kid. I end up meeting Nova, and we instantly hit it off. Cru wasn't happy at all, Nova had gotten pregnant with our daughter Star, and I was preparing to propose to her, but something happened that caused us to split up," I said.

"That was the video of Nova and ex NFL running back Delaunn Fleming who at the time played for the Tennessee Titans, right? I saw that he was suspended from the team after the revenge porn?" she asked. Now this hoe knew exactly what it was.

"Yeah that's it, I don't keep up with him but anyways, Cru and I got back together. Nova and I continued to co-parent, and it put a strain on my and Cru's relationship. Long story short, I had found out that Cru was involved with the Jonathan man since they were teenagers, and when he found out about us, he snapped and hurt her. In no way what he did was ok, but I also can't speak on how he felt being lied to and played by someone he loved. I realize Cru didn't have any family, so I will take care of the funeral cost, and my family and I ask for privacy during this time," I said ready to get this shit over with because ain't no telling what else she wanted to ask a nigga.

"Was it true that Crumari had planned on taking money from you, and that's really how you met? She had teamed up with Jonathan, but she ended up falling in love with you. We spoke with him this morning," Lacy asked. I didn't even know she knew about this shit, but that's her job to put a nigga on the spot.

"Yeah that's true, and that's why I broke up with her. I have a meeting to get to, but I hope I was able to answer all the questions you needed," I said, removing my mic. She signaled for the cameraman to turn the camera off.

"Did I say something you didn't like?" she asked.

"It's all good, but I wasn't aware that you had spoken to him, and I wasn't comfortable with that information being disclosed. When you gave me an opportunity to tell you what I didn't want the world to know, you should've told me that you were going to ask me that. But you got your interview, and I'm done talking. I have work to do so my assistant will see you guys out," I told her and excused myself

Novanna

"I CAN'T BELIEVE you guys got back together, but I'm happy for it all girl. And I'm so happy to see you're taking charge in here," Tammara said. I had gotten her number out of Muza's phone and invited her to the office to help a sister out.

"I'm just blessed. You know at times it still feels unreal, like any moment, I feel like somebody is gone pop up and cause some more damn drama. I swear every time Muza and I are back on good terms it happens," I told Tam.

"I think everything will be fine as long as neither of you has any more skeletons in the closet. Have you guys decided on a date yet?" Tam asked.

"Nah, I don't even need a date, and I don't want no huge ass wedding. I want a destination wedding with just us, my father, and Ms. Elizabeth," I admitted. It was something that I had been thinking about for a long time.

"Oh, hell no. I have to be in attendance because you will not find the perfect wedding dress without me," Tam joked.

"I was gone have you do that anyway, and of course you can come. My ass doesn't have any friends," I said and felt a little sad as I thought about Kelly.

"Why the sad look when you said that?" Tam asked me.

"I thought about my old roommate Kelly. She was the only person

I ever considered a real friend. That girl was like my sister. When she started dating Cru's boyfriend/brother, she changed," I said. Tam busted out laughing

"Bitch, you stupid! Boyfriend/brother?" she asked me.

"Yeah, they were brother and sister because the same foster family took them in, but that shit turned into a relationship. But yeah, she changed. He turned her into a weak bitch. She did so much stuff that I don't think I could forgive her for, especially between Muza and I. We're both mothers now, and that was something I always envisioned us doing together. Now she's got to raise her kid alone because Jon Jon killed Cru," I told Tam. She let out a huge sigh.

"Boy, I swear you guys' lives are so juicy. It sounds like it's made for TV," Tam said. The door to my office opened, and Muza walked in.

"Hey, baby, how did the interview go?" I asked.

"Sup Tam, and man it was just an interview. I rushed through that shit. Ain't too much they're gone get from it but Cru and our past, how she lied, and how we broke up. They brought up that tape shit about you and that jerk ass nigga," Muza said. I rolled my eyes. I thought that shit was behind me.

"Oh," was all I said.

'What y'all got going on?" he asked.

"Girl talk nothing major. We're talking about this destination wedding that I wanted to have," I threw out there so that he could catch it.

"Destination wedding, huh?" he replied.

"It would be nice. I really don't want a huge wedding. Plus, I want to hurry up and marry you before you change your mind," I joked.

"As long as you ain't got no more secrets, I ain't going nowhere," Muza said. I wanted to smack the hell out of him, and Tam was over there cracking up.

"Don't entertain this fool, girl. Get out. I have work to do. I have some people coming in for interviews. I've got to get some folks in this office because it sholl ain't gone run itself," I told Muza. Muza came around to my side of the desk and kissed me.

"I'm going to pick up Star and go over Malcolm's, so stop by when you finish up," he said.

"Ok love," I told him. I watched as he walked out of the office.

"Bitch, help me plan a wedding!" I yelled excitedly. I stood up and started twerking at the desk. I couldn't believe I was for real deal securing the bag and his heart now.

* * *

AFTER FIVE INTERVIEWS, I had hired a crew and was doing more interviews tomorrow. I was looking to bring on ten people to help me run Star Editorials. After finishing up, I grabbed my things so that I could get to my father's house. I really wanted to go to bed because I was tired. I had to get used to this working lifestyle, but I couldn't complain. I locked up everything and got on the elevator. When I stepped into the lobby, I asked the valet to bring my car around. I was ready to get out of these damn heels.

When my car came around, I removed my shoes and threw them bitches in the back seat. I looked at the time, and it was going on eight p.m., but it felt later than that. Before I pulled off, I texted Muza letting him know that I was on the way. I turned on the radio and jammed to the sounds of Toni Romiti and DC Young Fly new song "Never Thought" .

Never thought that I would give my all like this, but now I'm all in
Never thought I'd be sprung like this
Never thought I'd wanna have your kids
I never thought you could have my heart
Every night you got it, hope these feelings never fade
You touch my body, boy, in all the right places
We switch positions now we making' our bed shake
And now we're kissing' while we're making love faces

I WAS SO into the sound and singing to the top of my lungs because I was feeling this shit; whoever thought that DC Young Fly's crazy ass could sing.

After a nice twenty-minute drive, I pulled into my father driveway. I turned the car off and sat there for a while. I remember the day I first stepped foot here coming to visit my mother. Man, I missed my mommy so bad. In a way, I'm glad Malcolm was my dad because sometimes it felt like she was still here when I was around him. I knew that he really loved my mother, but he also loved Ms. Elizabeth. She was a sweet lady, and I was happy to have her in my life also. I came a long way. I could've still been escorting trying to make a quick buck if I hadn't of went to the Burberry store that day. I smiled and grabbed my purse. Excuse the ratchet moment I was about to have, but I left my shoes in the back seat and walked inside the house barefoot. When I walked in the house, all I heard was Surprise!!

MUZAINI

*W*e all stood in the living room waiting for Nova to arrive. I know that I had asked her to marry me before Cru had died that day in the office, but I wanted to do it right, and in front of our family because she did say once everything was taken care of, she would marry me. When she brought up the destination wedding, I looked at Tammara because I was hoping she didn't tell her about the surprise that I had set up.

I had the steps lit up with candles and white roses lining the steps. Everyone was dressed in white, including Star. She wasn't expecting a thing. When she walked into the house, everyone yelled surprise. I laughed because she jumped and looked around taking everything in. I think she was in a state a shock because it took her a long time to say something. The next thing I know she started crying. I walked over to her and closed the door.

"Baby, where your shoes at?" I asked while wiping the tears from her face.

"In the car. My damn feet were hurting. What is all of this, Muza?" she asked. My Uncle Malcolm and Aunt Elizabeth were standing over there along with Star, Darius, and Tammara.

"Come here," I said, taking her to the bottom step and sitting her down.

I grabbed her hand and removed the ring she had on her ring finger that I had already given her. Tammara walked over and handed me another box, taking the ring that I had. I got down on one knee.

"Nova, I know that I already gave you a ring, but I felt you deserved a new ring because we have been through so much, and I felt like that old ring was a thing of the past. I want to create new memories with you. I want everything to start off fresh as if we just met. Remember when we were playing life was a little easy then, but now, we are parents to a beautiful baby girl, and we must set the perfect example for her. You know I think God knew what he was doing keeping us apart. He knew then we might have kept saying we were ready for marriage, but we really weren't. You make me the happiest man on earth, well besides Star, she comes first. But, I can't wait to make you my wife, so again, I ask you Novanna Collier will you do me the honor of becoming Ms. Muhammad?" I asked her.

Man, Nova was crying her ass off. I ain't seen her cry this much ever.

"Muzaini, I would do anything you ask me to, and I most definitely will be your wife," she said. I slid the ring on her finger, and she wrapped her arms around me and continued to cry.

"Come on Nova with all this damn crying, girl," I said, and she started fanning her face.

"I can't help it. These last few days have just been overwhelming and exciting," she said.

"Well, I got another surprise," I told her, handing her an envelope. Nova opened the envelope.

"This can't be?" Nova asked, jumping up and down.

"Hell, when are we leaving? I'm ready to get y'all asses married!" Uncle Malcolm said. Everyone laughed.

"I have to call up my homie Fiyah that owns Cole Funeral Home. He's going to handle Cru's arrangements for me. I was really considering having her cremated since she doesn't have any family," I said.

"What you gone do with the ashes? I don't want that bad Juju around me," Nova said.

"She's got one cousin that I know of. I don't know if they blood related, but I can have my people reach out and see if she wants the ashes. I can have Cru cremated, and we hop on the next thing smoking out of here so that I can make you my wife," Muza said, looking at me.

"Make your calls then," Nova said, looking at her ring. I stepped out of the room, but not before stopping at Tammara.

"Can you try and get in touch with Cru's cousin Kesha?" I asked.

"Sure," she said.

Continuing out of the room, I called Fiyah. I knew he was still probably at work. That nigga lived for burning motherfuckers. Don't get me wrong he has a legit business. Matter of fact he and his wife, Desire, got two funeral homes. Besides the undertaker business, that nigga is an undertaker for the streets and some more illegal shit, but I try to stay away from all that.

"Yo Fiyah!" I yelled into the phone.

"Hold on," he said, turning the radio down.

"What's up, stranger? You big time now don't have time for motherfuckers that grew up with you," he said.

"Aw hell, here you go. Don't do me like that. I'm calling now," I said.

"Yeah nigga, probably because your ass needs something. So, what you want?" he asked.

"I need to make funeral arrangements for Cru. I really want something simple. Cremation and placed in an urn, well that's if her cousin says she wants her remains," I told him.

"Cool, I'll get Desire to contact the coroner and get her body," he said.

"Let me know the damage, and I got you. I'll stop by in the morning," I told him.

"That's what's up, nigga," Fiyah said.

I looked back in the room at my family. They all wore smiles on their faces and was enjoying the moment. I guess that was the code to life. Live every day and moment like it's your last because tomorrow is never promised.

ANGUILLA

NOVA

$\mathcal{W}$hen I stepped off the jet in Anguilla, I was in awe. Everything was so beautiful. I don't know what made Muza pick Anguilla for our destination wedding, but I was glad he did. It was hot. I looked at my phone, and it said it was 87 degrees. I wanted to get to the beach as soon as possible. We took a limo to the Four Seasons resort we were staying in.

"This place is so beautiful, baby," I told Muza.

"I knew you would like it. You know when we get to the hotel we have to go our separate way until tomorrow," he told me. I pouted

"Yes, I know. I can't wait to marry you tomorrow," I whispered into his ear.

"Lord, I wish you guys cut that out. You will have plenty of time for all that later," Ms. Elizabeth joked.

"I swear all y'all just a bunch of haters." I laughed. We arrived at the hotel, and that was another beauty. I swear this island was so beautiful. We entered the hotel, and Tammara walked off.

'Where is she going?" Ms. Elizabeth asked.

"She's making sure everything is situated for the wedding. She had a person she was working with to plan everything. I wanted a nice simple wedding, and I can't wait until you see what I'm wearing," I told Ms. Elizabeth.

"Oh Lord," Muza said, coming up behind us.

"Well ladies, this is our stop. You girls behave yourselves, and I'll see you tomorrow to make you my wife," he said, leaning in and kissing me passionately. I hated to see him leave, and I wanted to be up under his ass 24/7, but I knew the rules of the wedding. I watched as him, Darius, and my father headed towards their suite.

"Don't get any ideas. You know you don't have to worry about him doing anything crazy," Elizabeth said.

"I guess you're right," I told her.

We received our keys to the suite and headed upstairs. Once settled inside the room we popped open a bottle of champagne and sat around engaged in conversation.

"What did Muza end up doing to Cru?" Ms. Elizabeth asked. Cru was the last person I wanted to talk about the night before my wedding.

"His friend cremated her, and I don't know what he did with the remains because the girl that he asked if she wanted didn't want them," I told Elizabeth. Tammara walked in and plopped down on the couch.

"Ok, can I see my dress now, what if I don't like it?" I asked. Tammara said she had special something made for me since our wedding was on the beach, and I have yet to see or hear about the dress.

"I swear you are getting on my nerves about this damn dress," she said, walking over to a bag that was hanging up.

"Now this is from Israeli designer Alon Livne," she said unzipping the bag. Once she pulled the dress from the bag, a smile graced my face.

"Where is the rest of it?" Ms. Elizabeth asked.

"I love it, Tam!" I said, standing up and grabbing the dress.

"It's gone look even better once it's on. Go try it on," Tam said.

I headed to the bedroom and started to remove my clothes. Tam and Elizabeth came into the room to assist me. I stepped in the gown, and Tam zipped me up.

Lord I thought this was two pieces. The dress was called "Heaven" and it looked like heaven on my body. It really wasn't a dress. It was a flesh tone bodysuit/swimsuit that was jeweled out in the crotch, breasts, shoulders, and butt area. It had a white long flowing silk over-skirt connected at the hips, which flowed behind me. This shit was off the chain. It was different. It was beach and wedding ready. I looked at myself in the mirror, and I watched as a single tear rolled down my face.

Wedding Day

I stood there looking at Muza in his white linen short set. A single tear rolled down my face. I was extremely happy that this was finally about to take place. I was about to become this man's wife. My father stood beside me looking dapper as well. Holding my bouquet tight as hell, I knew it was time. Once the saxophone player started blowing in the saxophone, we took off down the aisle. I felt like I was walking in molasses, and the butterflies in my stomach weren't letting up. This mixed emotion shit I was going through was for the birds. A mixture of excitement, being impatient and scared all in one was a bit much. Then to see Muza crying, that shit took me out. It was a moment that I would forever remember and use against him. He looked nothing like this at he and Cru's "wedding". And you know what here we were on the beach with the sun shining, and he didn't have on no shades.

Muza stepped up and took my hand, placing it in his and giving my father a head nod. He leaned over and kissed my cheek.

"Ok, you can wait on the kisses," the officiant said.

Everyone laughed. As the officiant started the wedding, I got lost in Muzaini's eyes. I saw the first time we met, our first date, our first time, which conceived our daughter, I saw deep in his soul the love that he had for me and only me. We had overcome hell and high water to get to this point in our lives. I know once we are married we will face some more obstacles as we know relationships aren't perfect, but it's nothing that we couldn't handle together.

I heard Muza say, "I Do", snapping out of my trance. The officiant was now talking to me.

"I Do," I answered with a wide smile.

"You may now kiss your bride," he told Muza

Muza leaned in, grabbed my face, and we kissed. We held our kiss for I know five minutes— I ain't seen my boo all night. I was officially Mrs. Muzaini Muhamad.

We walked back down the aisle as the photographer took our pictures. I looked at the purple bouquet that I was holding and held it to the sky showing my mommy, who I wish was here sharing this moment. It was over, and I end up doing all that I set out to do, SECURING THE BAG AND HIS HEART TOO!!!

To whom this may concern.

THE DAY I MET MUZAINI, of course, we all know the intentions weren't good. Along with meeting him, my own life changed in so many ways. Dealing with the illness of my mother was hard for me, but finding out about my father was even worse. Through those hardships, the changes that came about were challenging. I had to deal with heartbreak, betrayal, becoming a mother, and trying to get my life together.

So much has happened and changed since Muzaini and I exchanged vows. We enjoyed our honeymoon for two whole weeks. It was much needed because when we got back to the city, it was go mode for me, and of course, Muza never stops his grind. We are thinking about more children, but that might come at a different time. Star has all our love for the time being.

I finally launched *Star Editorials,* and it is doing great. We have a physical magazine and online site. You guys probably want to know about the book I was working on, well you're reading it. Thank you, guys, so much for letting me share my journey because every happy ending wasn't perfect getting there.

Love,

Novanna Muhammad

FROM THE AUTHOR

I hope you guys enjoyed this series. I enjoyed writing it, especially book two. This work of art started off as a challenge then I was able to pick up like nothing happened and finish it. Check out some other reads by me.

A Savage and His Lady 1&2

Masking My Pain

Fiyah and Desire: Down to Ride for A Boss

Securing the Bag and His Heart

Securing the Bag and His Heart Too

Upcoming Reads

Remnants (Novella)

Fiyah and Desire: Still Down to Ride for A Boss

9 781722 074166